The thought of never taking a risk was messing with her head.

With the last sip of her margarita, she spotted a tall, gorgeous beast of a man. He was six foot two if he was an inch, all packed nicely into cowboy duds, boots and hat.

Maybe exactly what she needed was to bring one of these hunky cowboys home tonight. Preferably, that handsome beast making direct eye contact with her.

His incredible eyes never wavered. They stayed on her. And she returned his scrutiny, finding not a flaw on the sharp angles of his face, the set of his chiseled jaw or the deep ocean blue of his eyes.

He made her breath catch. He made her hot.

The silent communication between them was ready to combust.

* * *

The Texan Takes a Wife is part of the series Texas Cattleman's Club: Blackmail—No secret— or heart—is safe in Royal, Texas...

Dear Reader,

Welcome back to the Texas Cattleman's Club and Royal, Texas! I'm happy to say that romance is in the autumn air and my Thanksgiving story starring Erin Sinclair and Daniel Hunt will bring a cornucopia of love and intrigue and mystery.

Erin Sinclair isn't a risk taker. At least, she never has been, but a past scandal in her hometown of Seattle has her thinking outside the box lately. When she climbs up on a mechanical bull to prove to herself and the world she's no wilting willow, the ride she takes knocks her on her butt. In comes a rugged cowboy to save the day, and Erin's soon engaged in another kind of ride, one that leaves her just as breathless...with Daniel Hunt.

If you're an animal lover, you'll soon meet Daniel's menagerie—the big hunky beast of a man brings home wounded strays to his ranch on a regular basis. One night, after a hit-and-run, he enlists Erin to help bring an injured animal to safety, and soon the half collie, half German shepherd named Lucky sneaks his way into Erin's and Daniel's hearts.

But there's a cyber culprit on the loose and Erin and Daniel get swept up in the investigation. Finding and bringing to justice Maverick, the mysterious bully who has caused so much heartache and pain to the Texas Cattleman's Club members, is a must.

Wishing you happy reading and a wonderful holiday season!

Charlene Sands

CHARLENE SANDS

THE TEXAN TAKES A WIFE

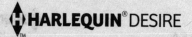

Special thanks and acknowledgment are given
to Charlene Sands for her contribution to the
Texas Cattleman's Club: Blackmail miniseries.

Recycling programs
for this product may
not exist in your area.

ISBN-13: 978-0-373-83878-3

The Texan Takes a Wife

HARLEQUIN®
™ www.Harlequin.com

Printed in U.S.A.

Charlene Sands is a *USA TODAY* bestselling author of more than forty romance novels. She writes sensual contemporary romances and stories of the Old West. When not writing, Charlene enjoys sunny Pacific beaches, great coffee, reading books from her favorite authors and spending time with her family. You can find her on Facebook and Twitter, write her at PO Box 4883, West Hills, CA 91308, or sign up for her newsletter for fun blogs and ongoing contests at charlenesands.com.

Books by Charlene Sands

Harlequin Desire

Moonlight Beach Bachelors

Her Forbidden Cowboy
The Billionaire's Daddy Test
One Secret Night, One Secret Baby
Twins for the Texan

The Slades of Sunset Ranch

Sunset Surrender
Sunset Seduction
The Secret Heir of Sunset Ranch
Redeeming the CEO Cowboy

The Worths of Red Ridge

Carrying the Rancher's Heir
The Cowboy's Pride
Worth the Risk

Texas Cattleman's Club: Blackmail

The Texan Takes a Wife

Visit her Author Profile page at Harlequin.com, or charlenesands.com, for more titles.

This story is dedicated to the little munchkins in my life who make every holiday wonderful and exciting.

With love to my special girls—Everley, Kyra, Madyson and Lila Dawn.

One

Some of her friends had bucket lists, things they wanted to do before they kicked it, but Erin Sinclair had a list of Never Do's and riding a mechanical bull in an arena of highly capable-to-the-bone Texans was one of them. The legless, leather-clad metal bull scared her silly as it jerked around, keeping only the most proficient on its back.

Yet as she sipped her second Cadillac margarita in the Dark Horse Saloon outside the Royal city limits the thought of never doing it, never taking a risk, was messing with her head.

She'd broken from the pack of women she'd come here with, half a dozen welcoming ladies from the Texas Cattleman's Club who'd befriended her and invited her to a birthday party at the Dark Horse.

Now the party was over and all of those women had gone home to their boyfriends or husbands. Erin had neither. It was November and she'd be heading back to her hometown in Seattle the first of the year, without having done anything Texan, anything remotely wild.

"Ready for another, blondie?" the bartender asked, his gaze on the near-empty glass in her hand, yet it was the dubious look in his eyes that brought her five-foot-four frame to attention. "Or maybe you've had enough?"

"I haven't had nearly enough," she said. "One more." She offered him a sweet smile. "Thank you."

The bartender walked away shaking his head and she focused back on the bull that seemed to be calling to her. Was she being an idiot, or was that bull looking straight at her, tempting her to take a chance, teasing her with his grotesque fake horns to come get him?

With the last sip of her margarita at her lips, she spotted a tall, gorgeous beast of a man. He was six foot two if he was an inch, all packed nicely into cowboy duds, boots and hat, his shoulders wide enough to carry that longhorn over his shoulders without breaking a sweat.

Speaking of Never Do's: in all her twenty-six years, she'd never done a Texan before. She burst into a fit of giggles. Good thing no one around her noticed or she'd really look like an idiot. But the sad fact was, there were also forty-eight other states' worth of men she hadn't been with. Her home state of Washington housed her ex, Rex Talbot. Now, he was a piece of work. And she was glad she was staying in Royal, Texas, at least for the holidays. Rex had nearly ruined her reputation in Seattle, but she wasn't going to dwell. Not tonight.

Maybe exactly what she needed was to bring one of these hunky cowboys home tonight. Preferably, that chunk of handsome beast making direct eye contact with her. He had perfected the art of smolder, had it down to a science and she was loving all the attention and the fact that he'd picked her out of a sea of stunning women.

His incredible eyes never wavered. They stayed on her. And she returned his scrutiny, finding not a flaw on the sharp angle of his face, the set of his chiseled jaw or the deep ocean blue of his eyes.

He made her breath catch. He made her yearn. He made her hot. The silent communication between them was ready to combust.

Sheesh, maybe she shouldn't have another margarita. She was really thinking outside the box tonight. She turned to the bartender to tell him to forget that last one. She didn't need it.

And when she turned back around, ready for another round of eye contact with her handsome broad-shouldered Texan, he had disappeared. She searched for him, desperate to find him, scanning the entire saloon with eyes peeled, but it was no use. She'd lost him in the swarm of the crowd. He may have gotten bored and left the saloon.

Disappointed, her stomach clenched. Story of her life.

So much for taking a risk.

But then, there was always the mechanical bull.

Yes, that's exactly what she'd do. She'd ride the darn thing. Why not? She needed one lasting memory to take back with her to Seattle. One thing she could say she'd conquered while in Texas. The ex-nanny, a woman who also knew her way around a music room filled with children, might just need this bit of excitement to cling to once she left the lone star state.

Ha!

And suddenly, that bull didn't look so intimidating anymore. Suddenly, the challenge bolstered her courage. She could do this. She could ride that silly-looking contraption. And her bravado didn't waver while she stood in line to take her turn. It didn't waver when one rider after another eventually got tossed off. Just a few seconds, was all she was asking. Five. Five seconds on that bull, and she'd be satisfied, and thrilled and proud.

"You can do this," she muttered under her breath.

And when it was her turn, the arena host whose booming voice rose above the patrons of the saloon announced, "This little lady is Erin from Seattle, and she's gonna give Destroyer a go."

She gulped and a crewman helped her up onto the leather back of the bull. "We'll take it slow," he said. "Use your thighs as a grip and try to keep yourself centered as the bull begins to move."

Once he moved back, she took a big breath and nodded to the crewman to start up the robot.

And the bull began to jerk.

Erin looked up into the dazzling blue eyes of the beast. He was kneeling over her, staring at her face, a frown pulling his very kissable mouth down. Had she slept through her very best fantasy? What was going on? She moved and the cushioned padding at her back rebelled with a squeak. "What the..."

"You took a fall," he said in a deep baritone voice. With a nod of his head, he gestured to the metal bull.

She realized where she was instantly. And that the crowd circling the arena was watching her. "How long did I ride?"

That brought a smile to his lips. Oh, and it was a killer. "About three seconds."

She grimaced.

"Your head?" he asked.

When a crewman approached, the beast gave him a glare that would have sent the Hulk cowering away.

"I feel fine," she answered. She did. She'd been tossed off the bull and landed hard on the padding, but nothing hurt, nothing seemed fuzzy. *Anymore.*

Except that her handsome beast was at her side, helping her to her feet. She was met with a round of applause and cheers. She chuckled out of sheer embarrassment and then her body tilted, swaying sideways and everybody else seemed to be leaning. "Uh-oh."

"I've got ya," he said, catching her before she lost her balance and lifting her into his arms. "You need air."

She stared up at him again, amazed at his strength. From this angle, he was even more appealing. His size, the sexy base of his throat, the scruff on his face and those blue eyes, locked him into a category all his own. He carried her as if she was a handful of marshmallows, instead of a twenty-six-year-old woman. And before they got too far, she pointed toward the bar. "My purse."

He nodded and changed directions, carrying her over to swoop up her purse off the bar stool with the grace of a panther. He glanced down for a second. "I'm Dan."

She smiled. What an odd way to meet. But she was not complaining. "I'm Erin. Nice to meet you."

He grunted a reply.

The contrast of the dimly lit smoke-filled noisy saloon to the cool crisp fall Texas air outside helped to wake her up out of this steamy sort of dream she was in. She didn't want Dan to put her down, but it was awkward and she didn't know where to put her arms, so she'd looped them around his neck. Now that they were outside, touched by moonlight and facing the parking lot where it was quieter, the reality of the situation was starting to dawn on her. "I, uh, I'm fine now," she said. "You can put me down."

He gave her another glance, nodded and then took great care to allow her to slide down his body. For safety's sake, she assumed, but oh, the brush of his body with hers sent all the right signals and she shivered.

"Cold?" he asked.

"No," she answered. "I'm, uh, this is silly. I hardly know you, but..."

She couldn't finish her thought. Was she about to tell this gorgeous cowboy that just a brush of his body to hers made her tingle from head to toe? No, she couldn't do that.

"Got it," he said, and without any discussion at all, he seemed to know. Oh God. How embarrassing. Did women fall at his feet like this all the time?

"So why the bull?" he asked.

"Because it was there," she answered immediately.

His brows furrowed. He didn't get her little joke.

She tried to explain, "It's just that, I'm from Seattle, staying in Texas for the holidays and I wanted to do something Texan. You know," she added quickly, remembering her thought a while ago about doing *him*. "I mean we don't have a lot of mechanical bulls in Washington."

"I don't suppose." Still, the furrow.

"And I... Well, you see my nanny job brought me here. And then a few friends I'd made invited me to a birthday party tonight at the Dark Horse, so I tagged along with them, but they all went home, and I wanted..."

He was a good listener, but he wasn't adding much to the conversation. And she wasn't going to babble on anymore. "Never mind."

Talk about the strong silent type. He was that and so much more.

"You sober enough to drive home?" he asked.

"Oh, uh, yes. I stopped drinking a while ago. I'm feeling fine now, aside from the humiliation."

He stared at her for what seemed like a minute, his eyes flickering over her mouth and in that heated moment, she wanted nothing more but to lock lips with him, to taste his whisky breath and feel the absolute thrill of kissing him. Almost as if he heard her thoughts, his mouth cocked up and he drew a long breath.

And then he said, "I'll walk you to your car."

Disappointment that the stranger who'd just rescued her didn't want to kiss her into oblivion, she said, "Okay."

In a few minutes she'd be headed back to her guest cabin at the Flying E, with no job, no prospects, and trying to find a productive way to spend the next month or so. Her job being little Faye's nanny had ended when her employer Will Brady had found love here in Texas. And apparently, scandal-plagued grade school music teachers were not in hot demand, apparently in Seattle or anywhere else for that matter.

She pointed to her car. "It's just over there."

She could dream of a goodbye kiss from the stranger. Or she could give him one herself. It was risky, but she was warming to the idea. Executing it would be a different—

A car came to a screeching halt, right in front

of them on the street. Then a loud yelp rang out and something hit the pavement with a thud. And a dog began to whimper. The sound of his pained cries curled her stomach and she glanced at Dan. He didn't waste a second. He grabbed her hand and took off running toward the downed animal. The car sped off, the driver not even giving the poor animal a glance. Dan was at the dog's side immediately, kneeling beside him, cradling his head. "You'll be alright, boy," he said, whispering confidently near the dog's face as he began a thorough scan over his body. His big hands were gentle as he probed. He found a few gashes on the dog's backside where blood was beginning to pool. "You need some patching up, is all."

"Are you a vet?" she asked, noting the care he took with the animal.

"No, but he needs one. He's scared, probably in shock. That A-hole just drove off after hitting him."

Erin couldn't believe it, either. It was heartless and cold. She wished she could've gotten a look at the license plate.

The dog looked to be a mix of collie and German shepherd with big round brown eyes. He watched Dan carefully, giving him blind trust. "Will you stay with him?" Dan asked, sparing her a brief glance. "I have a blanket in my car."

"Sure, of course."

Dan rose and Erin took over his position. "You're gonna be just fine, pretty boy," she said, carefully stroking the dog just above the eyes. She made massage circles and the dog's whimpers stopped as his eyes drifted closed. He wore no collar and there was no way to contact his owner, if he even had one. Why had he been wandering out so late at night?

"That's it, boy. Rest. We're going to get you all fixed up."

Dan was back in an instant, and immediately tucked the blanket under the dog, careful not to cause him injury. The blanket was thick enough to absorb the little bit of blood at the wound site. "Bleeding isn't too bad."

"That's good, right?"

He nodded.

"What can I do to help?"

"You mind watching him in the backseat of my SUV? My vet is gonna meet me at my house. It's closer than his office."

"Sure," she said, stroking the dog's golden coat gently. "Of course I will."

And once Dan got her situated in the backseat of his car, the big blanketed dog scooted next to her and planted his sweet mug on her lap. Thatta boy. She smiled and continued to massage the dog's head, just over the eyes and occasionally stroking over his ears.

Dan didn't say much as he drove, but he kept glancing in the rearview mirror to see how the dog was doing. She was touched by his concern, the kindness in his eyes.

"Pretty nice vet to come out in the middle of the night for this sweet guy," she said.

Dan nodded, and she didn't think he'd say any-thing but seconds later, he admitted, "I do business with him at my ranch. He's a neighbor."

So Dan really was a cowboy. "Is it far?"

"Five more minutes."

And a short time later, Dan pulled into one of the garages of a beautifully appointed two-story estate. It was dark; she couldn't see more than what the ground lights surrounding the property gave away, but her instincts told her this ranch was massive and successful.

"I'll set up a bed in the kitchen and then come get him," Dan said.

Lights flicked on in the garage as he entered his home and Erin waited patiently. The dog was breathing heavily, but other than that, his whimpers from earlier were all gone. Thank goodness. Erin had never owned a dog, but back in her college days she used to walk dogs to pick up extra spending cash, and she'd grown fond of the species, even as she was also picking up their poop. She was sure this big guy would've stolen her heart too. He had those kind of eyes that seemed to touch her deep inside.

Once Dan came back, he removed the dog from the backseat, lifting him with as much care as he'd lifted her from the mat after her mechanical bull fiasco. Erin followed him inside to a kitchen a chef would envy. Despite the ivory cabinets, black gran-ite countertops trailing with gold vein, contempo-rary appliances and stone fireplace, the room looked cozy and lived-in.

Dan set the dog down and stroked him lovingly a few times. Then he grabbed a towel he'd soaked with warm water and began dabbing at the animal's wounds.

"You came up with that bed really fast," she said, kneeling beside Dan, curious about this man. "I'm impressed."

He shrugged. "I sorta rescue animals."

"You do?"

"Not deliberately."

"How does that work?"

"If strays come by, they end up staying. One I found stranded by the side of the road, another was left behind after the family moved out of Texas. The cats are all freeloaders. They kept coming around searching for food and I fed them."

"How many pets do you have?"

"Four dogs, three cats, a string of horses."

"Is this a horse farm?"

He shook his head. "Cattle ranch."

"Lots and lots of cattle, I assume."

His lips quirked up a bit. "Something like that."

Erin could easily imagine Dan surrounded by animals. He was one of those men that appeared tough on the outside, but she didn't doubt he was a total softie on the inside. When the dog was hit, Dan went into action mode, seeing to the injured animal's needs immediately.

Sort of like how he'd come to her rescue with the bull.

A few minutes later, Dan's neighbor, a man he

introduced as Doug Bristol, walked into the kitchen armed with his medical bag. He quickly went to work on the dog, giving him a thorough visual examination along with poking and prodding him gently in a few places. "He's lucky," he said after his exam. "He got pretty banged up, but nothing seems broken."

They watched the vet administer pain meds to the dog and then bandage his wounds. When he'd done all he could for him, Dr. Bristol told Dan to bring him by his office in the morning. "I want to examine him again. What's his name?"

Dan shrugged, then said, "How about we call him Lucky?"

Dan gave his neighbor a nod. "Lucky."

"Okay, I'll see Lucky, then, tomorrow. Nice to meet you, Erin."

"Thanks for stopping by, Doc," Dan said, and the two men shook hands.

After seeing his neighbor to the door, Dan walked back into the kitchen and there was stony silence. Now that the dog was sleeping and seemed fine, there was no reason for her stay any longer. Awkward moments passed as both of them stared at each other. "I should go," she whispered. "You managed two rescues in one night. You must be tired."

"Not tired, are you?"

She shook her head. She couldn't believe how easily she'd done that, knowing full well if she'd said she was tired, Dan would've driven her back to the Dark Horse to pick up her car. "No, I'm not tired. Kinda keyed up after what happened tonight."

Perhaps admitting that to Dan was the riskiest thing she'd done all night.

"Yeah, me too. Cup of coffee? Something stronger?"

No more alcohol for her tonight. She wasn't quite sure if it was the mechanical bull or the two Cadillac margaritas she'd had earlier that landed her flat on her ass at the saloon. "Coffee sounds perfect."

And the man of few words set about making coffee.

Erin sipped Dan's coffee and nibbled on a warm giant chocolate-chip cookie oozing with melted chocolate. Warming the cookies before gobbling them down was her mother's trick, and tonight Erin put it to the test. A few seconds in the microwave made even a stale cookie speak to the senses.

"Aren't they good warm?" Erin asked Dan.

He nodded. "Good."

Instead of Gorgeous Beast, maybe she should call him Caveman. The man seemed to have perfected the art of grunting, nodding and giving one-word answers. But his eyes spoke volumes and right now she was the object of his intense smolder. Not that she was complaining. He was almost as delicious as the cookie that was coating the interior of her mouth with chocolate goodness.

"So how long have you lived here?"

"In Texas? All my life," he said.

"I'm from Seattle."

He sipped coffee. "So you said."

"I did? When?"

"After the bull tossed you off."

"Oh yeah. That bull thing was a dumb idea."

He nodded, a smile lifting the corners of his mouth. "Kinda courageous."

"Really?" She perked up. Had he just complimented her?

"But not real smart." He tossed the last of his cookie in his mouth.

She rolled her eyes and he laughed, a big hearty he-man sound that did things to her sanity. "I really should go. Would you mind calling me a cab?"

He stood. "I'll drive you."

"But you shouldn't leave Lucky alone."

Dan gave the sleeping dog a glance. "He's getting the rest he needs. I doubt he'll wake up before morning."

But she suspected it was more than that. Dan was the kind of Texan bred with incredible manners and he wasn't about to send her off alone in the dead of night. He'd see her safely back to her car. "Only if you're sure."

"I'm not sure I want you to leave," he said quite candidly. "But I am sure about driving you."

Wow. Not only did he surprise her by speaking in full sentences, but he admitted he wanted her to stay longer. "Thank you. I'll take you up on that ride."

Dan nodded, appearing neither relieved nor disappointed.

She really wanted to stay, but her risk-taking skills were momentarily disabled. "You know, I don't think I ever thanked you for saving my pride and my hide this evening. It was really kind of you." She reached up and planted a kiss to his scruffy, super sexy cheek.

Just as she was backing away, a strong arm wrapped about her waist, drawing her against the wall of his chest. He was massive, in a very good sort of way, and an image of him shirtless muscled its way into her head.

"I need to thank you too," he said.

"For?" Trapped against him, her breath hitched. This was different from before when he'd carried her out of the Dark Horse Saloon. This was more intimate. They were alone in Dan's big ranch house. Two consenting adults.

"Helping with Lucky." Using his thumb, he tilted her chin up until she met his striking blue eyes. Oh boy. He was going to kiss her and she gave him a nonverbal okay. He took his time, inching closer to her mouth. And he was taking forever. The anticipation was killing her.

Then his mouth came down on hers and her lids lowered. She fell into the delicious, fiery, heaven-help-her, hot, hot kiss. The taste of chocolate and coffee mixed with sheer raw passion. Having his lips on hers blew her away. It was like a force of nature, something powerful and inspiring. She roped her arms around his neck and he circled her waist, connecting them, freeing them to continue whatever this was.

Dan's mouth became more demanding and little throaty sounds pressed from her lips as she indulged. Their tongues mated and Dan let out a grunt of approval that made her smile inside. Her hands threaded through his dark blond hair, the strands curling up at the collar of his shirt. She stood incredibly close to his rock hard body and it was difficult not to notice the state of his arousal. She found herself in the same situation—*wanting*.

Wanting to stay.

Wanting more time with him.

Wanting to take a risk with this tall Texan.

And just as those thoughts were cementing in her head, Dan ended the kiss and backed away. "Sorry." He shrugged. "I got carried away."

She smiled, missing his lips on her, missing his warmth and heat. "That's my line. I got carried away. By you, back at the saloon."

"I didn't plan on bringing you here."

"I know. It was just Lucky, I guess." She giggled at her own joke and even the big man smiled.

"You think so?" He pulled her back into his arms. "'Cause I was feelin' lucky just a minute ago."

She stared at his mouth. "It's been a long time since I felt this lucky," she said softly. He furrowed his brows again, something he did often. She found that trait incredibly appealing.

"Same here, Erin. Will you stay the night?"

She nodded, murmuring a soft, "Yes."

Then without another word, Dan took her shaky hand and led her out of the kitchen.

He liked Erin. If he was being honest, probably too damn much, and it had been a long while since he met a woman who sparked his interest. He'd spotted her at the Dark Horse, and almost instantly there was a connection. And also almost instantly, he knew she didn't belong in the saloon. When she'd climbed up on that mechanical bull, he figured she was in for the ride of her life. For a few seconds, that is. But as soon as the bull tossed her off, he'd come running to her rescue, shielding her embarrassment, making eye contact with the crowd, daring anyone to laugh as he carried her off.

What was it about him? He rescued animals and damsels in distress, or so it seemed. Bringing her to his cattle ranch at Hunt Acres had never been his plan, but then the dog was hit by a car and all of a sudden, they were here together in the middle of the night and now she was on his bed, reaching for him.

It was damn hard to think straight *or at all.*

He lowered onto the bed, taking her into his arms and kissed her again, careful not to crush her small frame. She was sweet and sexy and willing. Was he the risk she'd decided to take tonight too? He had to make certain this was what she wanted, had to give her a way out. "Are you sure, Erin?"

Her pretty blue-green eyes darkened. It was heady stuff seeing her nod and murmur, "Yes, I'm sure." Then she chewed her lower lip and added, "Aren't you?"

Her question caught him off guard. He nearly laughed, but held back. Didn't she know how much he wanted this? He'd picked her out of a crowd at the Dark Horse, hadn't been able to take his eyes off the sweet blonde in tight jeans and a gold blouse the exact shade of her pretty hair. A woman who'd appeared completely out of her element. She'd intrigued him from the get-go.

Now she was in his bed. "Absolutely."

Relieved, her expression softened.

"You didn't really doubt that, did you?"

She smiled, a stunner that made his body go completely rigid. He was through talking and ready to give Erin a much better ride than she'd had on that bull.

Erin was taking a risk, making a memory she'd bring back to Seattle when her time in Texas was up. She wasn't going to dwell. She wasn't going to admonish herself. She was all in. Dan's size thrilled her. He towered over her, all brawn and muscle, solid and sure, yet his touch was tender. She placed incredible trust in this man already. She loved his hands on her, his fingertips caressing her face as he kissed her. She responded to him carnally, soft murmurs of approval and pleasure parting her lips.

Dan kissed a path down her throat, his hot breath searing the slope of her breasts. In just a second, he had her blouse unbuttoned and his mouth moved over her, teasing her nipples to rosy points. She moaned, relishing the laps of his tongue on her skin. Her bra disappeared magically, Dan's talent making her head spin. She loved this feeling of being loose, unbridled and unaware of anything but the man spreading heat and excitement through her body.

Her zipper was down, her jeans pulled off and Dan was there, cupping her panties in his large palm. The warmth seared through her, the pressure unbelievably perfect. He lay beside her on the bed, making her dreams come true. And just then, she stopped, a coherent thought pressing through the pleasure. His shirt was still on. He was fully clothed and that just wasn't fair. She needed to touch him, to make him lose all thought the way he was doing to her. She needed her hands on him and pulled at the snaps of his shirt. They opened easily, and with his help wrestled him out of his shirt.

Oh wow. His shoulders, squared and broad, were massive in size. There was just so much of him to touch and she didn't hesitate. She laid her palms on him and his eyes shuttered closed. "Sweetness," he rasped.

She explored eagerly, sinking her hands over his taut muscles, the ripped cords of his skin and lower still until she met with the fine hairs below his torso.

His erection pulsed against her.

"Dan," she murmured, and pressed over the bulge.

"Hang on, woman." He gritted.

Instantly, she was on her back again, his one

hand tying her wrists above her head, while the other worked her panties down her legs. When he touched her folds, her eyes squeezed shut and her hips arched. The strokes of his fingers were like music, each one bringing her to sighs and moans and desperate whimpers. He played her sweetly and then the strokes came stronger, harder and her breaths hitched higher and higher.

She was ready. So ready.

She cried out, her release overpowering. And Dan was there, kissing her, stroking her hair and making it all so much better. She came down slowly and dared to look in his eyes.

They were dazzling, gleaming and hungry.

"That was a beautiful thing," he whispered.

She had to agree.

She'd poked the bear and he wouldn't be denied. Thank goodness.

He kicked off his boots and she reached for his belt buckle. He was all too willing to help her divest him of his clothes.

Naked now, Dan's raw power excited her all over again. His beauty lay in his solid strength, his massive frame, the tenderness in how he made love and as she gazed below his waist for the first time, she took a big gulp of air.

Dan caught her eyeing him and concern wrinkled the corners of his eyes. He said so much in his expression and she heard him loud and clear in the nonverbal way he seemed to like to communicate.

Relieving him of any worry, she rained kisses on him again and tucked her body under him.

Her explanation went a long way in making him understand and he wasted no time in searching through his jeans to pluck out a condom. Then he rose onto his knees, this beautiful man towering above her and the image seared her brain, not to ever be forgotten. Ready now, she pulled him down and dipped her tongue into his mouth. It was heady to be the aggressor, to show him how much she wanted him, to hear him groan and whisper her name.

Dan took over from there and she followed his lead as he feather-touched her breasts until she was ready to scream, nudged her legs apart, grabbed on to her hips and guided himself home.

Two

Erin opened her eyes thirty minutes later and found herself alone in Dan's king-size bed. Her entire body was one sweetly serene sigh. If only she could bottle that feeling and keep it close, she'd be satisfied forever. It was truly luck and her clumsy attempt at the bull that brought her here, to Dan. She smiled and rolled over and came face-to-face with a gray-and-white fur-ball of fluff. "Hello," she said to the cat sitting in a regal pose on the nightstand beside the bed. "Who are you?"

The cat blinked several times.

She chuckled. "A big talker, I see. Just like your owner. So where do you suppose he is?"

She didn't wait for the cat's reply. She grabbed

Dan's shirt from the floor, laced her arms through the sleeves and fastened a few snaps.

She rose to check out her appearance in the mirror and was happy she didn't find a bad case of bed head. Considering how often Dan had run his hands through her hair, she took it as a good sign and strode out of the room. As she made her way down the hallway, she was met with a cocker spaniel mix of some sort with short stubby legs who was doing his best to keep up with her. The dog was much too animated for this time of night. As she reached the top of the stairs, she looked into the soulful eyes of a friendly black Lab. Friendly, she assumed, because his tail had started wagging as soon as he spotted her.

"You're a pretty one," she said, giving the dog a pat on the head. Then she made her way down the stairs with her entourage following behind.

She entered the kitchen and found Lucky sound asleep on his cozy bed. He was just as they'd left him, dozing calmly, and it did her heart good to see him resting. Then her gaze drifted to the other end of the room, where she noticed Dan by the counter, filling a bowl of fresh water for the dog. His concern for Lucky was touching and incredibly sweet, but nothing, and she meant *nothing*, compared to how her breath caught at the sight of him.

The dim kitchen light illuminated his very tanned, very bare chest, the dip of his low-slung black jeans and the sharp, almost too rugged planes on his face. Handsome to a fault, she thought. She wrapped her arms around her middle, suddenly a bit shy. "Hi."

He strode over to her, his eyes narrowed on the shirt she wore that touched her midthigh. His brows lifted in an approving way. "Hi."

Then his hands came to her waist and he gave a little tug, drawing her closer, and kissed her softly on the lips. Her shyness disappeared and she smiled. "Checking on Lucky?"

"Yep."

"How's he doing?"

"Seems fine," he answered, never taking his eyes off her. "I like you in my shirt."

"Oh, um, I hope you don't mind."

"Hell no, I don't mind." He dipped his head to meet her eyes and gave her waist a squeeze. "Everything okay?"

"Mmm, everything's fine," she assured him. "I met some of your friends." She pointed to the two dogs sniffing around Lucky's bed. The cat began rubbing her cheek up against the edge of the bed tentatively, wary of the sleeping animal she had yet to meet.

"That small cocker spaniel lapping around is Buggy. This big guy is Rio," and just as he offered that, the black Labrador sat down beside him and nuzzled Dan's leg.

"What about the cat?" she asked.

"That'd be Juliet."

"Juliet?"

"Yep, Romeo is probably sawing logs right now with the others."

"You have quite a family here."

"I suppose I'm the Pied Piper of stray animals."

"And of stray women?"

Dan blinked. "No, never have gathered stray women, Erin. I don't think of you that way."

She set her palms flat on his chest and his gasp filled the silent room. "I'm very glad about that."

"Are you?" His eyes flickered and moved over her body lazily, as if physically touching her again, as if thinking of new ways to please her.

Goodness, she was asking for trouble.

He bunched the material of her shirt in his hand and slowly tugged her closer. "I like you touching me," he rasped, his voice deep and low.

She gulped down a big noisy breath. Her body immediately transformed from sated and relaxed to crazy tingling bouts of tremors. She moved her hands on him, her fingertips grazing over his pecs, and her breathing sped up.

He let her shirt drop and reached up to cup her face in his hands, his eyes two dark pools of deep blue. "You want this?"

He didn't have to say it, again. She knew what he was asking. "Yes. I want you. Do y—"

"Just for the record, sweetness," he interrupted. "The answer is hell yes."

She barely had time to smile before his mouth came down on hers and she was being lifted off her feet, his big hands holding her cheeks from behind. Automatically her legs came around his waist and she clung on to him. Her core pressed against the rigid length of his erection. The impact had her moaning and Dan too was affected. A guttural groan coming from somewhere deep in his gut, sounded in her ears. They were lost in each other, mouths wet and hot and devouring.

He strode forward until her back was against the wall. "Like this?" he asked.

"I've never… Yes."

He crushed another kiss to her mouth and as soon as she opened to take a much-needed breath, he dipped his tongue inside and a hot spiraling fire erupted, melting her bones. Sensation after sensation ripped through her body. She was so ready for him, she could hardly stand it. It was amazing how much she craved being with Dan. He couldn't have done anything more, said anything better to her, than he wanted her again and again and again.

An awkward second passed as Dan maneuvered his jeans down and sheathed himself and then, he was nudging her entrance, his large hands driving her body closer, into him, until he was there again. Thrusting into her, silky hot tension grew stronger and stronger. He fit her and she fit him and it was the very best. She matched his pace, absorbing the bulk and feel of him as he gave her his heat.

She opened her eyes to see the gritty determination on his face, the carnal lust that belied his tender lovemaking from before. She relished each move, each explosive thrust of their joining. His hair was slicked back, curling at his nape, his eyes nearly closed, his mouth grinding out curse words she could barely hear, words that normally would shock her, but now only served to heighten her pleasure.

Her body seized tight, sensitized by each potent thrust. Each calculated move shot her closer and closer to the brink. "Dan," she called out.

"I'm right here, sweetness." He gritted out the words. "Don't hold back."

And it was the pleasured pain in his voice and not the words themselves that caused her to shatter, pulsing out a release so strong her body began to tremble. Dan held her tight and joined her, squeezing out every last ounce of power he possessed.

They stayed joined for a long moment, clinging to each other, holding on to something that would never be equaled. At least it was the case for her.

And finally, once their breathing slowed and their bodies cooled, Dan whispered, "Let's go to bed." He kissed her lightly on the mouth and carried her up the stairs.

Erin woke up before dawn. She'd gotten very little sleep during the night and as the big man beside her rolled over to spoon her, she smiled at his light snoring. She could stay in his arms all day, naked as she was, and drift peacefully in and out of sleep. But she wouldn't be the woman he couldn't get rid of in the morning. She knew how these things worked. She'd stay through morning coffee and then take off.

Dan obviously had a ranch to run, and she had… well, she didn't have her job as nanny anymore, since Will Brady had fallen deeply in love and little Faye soon would have a loving stepmother in Amberley Holbrook. She couldn't fault them their new future.

She'd been hired in Seattle and when Will was summoned to Royal to find Maverick—the creep who'd been harming good upstanding members of the Texas Cattleman's Club by spreading their secrets and blackmailing them via the internet—Erin had taken the trip with him to help out with Faye. Caring for the baby had been a blessing and being her nanny had helped Erin heal, or at the very least distracted her from the pain of Rex's betrayal. Sweet, busy little Faye had kept Erin on her toes. In the very best way.

Erin didn't know too much regarding the facts in the case Will was working on, but this Maverick guy seemed to be wrecking people's lives. Will's help here in Texas had been essential.

Her boss had been generous in paying her salary until the end of the year so she could stay on at the guest quarters of the Flying E Ranch until the time she'd have to return to her studio apartment in Seattle. And recently, her thoughtful employer had had a keyboard delivered to the cabin too, so Erin could continue playing music when she felt like it. Up until this point, she hadn't the heart to play again.

She was hoping the scandal with Rex Talbot that nearly ruined her reputation would've blown over by now and she had vowed to never put herself in such a vulnerable position again.

And if that meant saying goodbye this morning to Dan she-didn't-even-know-his-last-name, she'd do it. If he was interested in her, he'd have to make the first move.

Erin gently unclamped Dan's arm from about her waist and slowly sat up in bed. Last night, Dan had been adept in popping each of the snaps on the shirt she wore, insisting they both sleep in the buff, promising her he'd keep her warm. She had no doubt he would and sure enough all during the night he'd kept her cradled in the heat of his big beautiful body.

Giving the sleeping man another glance, she sighed and plucked up her clothes from the floor and then tiptoed into the master bathroom to shower.

She was sore in all the right places and the warm spray eased some of the aches. She hadn't had such a vigorous night of sex in forever. Once she was cleaned up and dressed in her street clothes, she ambled down the hallway with Buggy and another little runt of a dog—this one looked more like a poodle mix than anything else—following behind. She entered the kitchen, finding Lucky awake. She went to him and crouched down. "Hey, boy. How're you doing this morning?"

The dog's tail began to wag. Relieved he was looking much better, she stroked his coat a few times and the dog's wet tongue came out to lap at her hand. Sweet. Lucky was truly lucky he'd been rescued and taken care of by Dan.

After petting the dog, she set about making coffee. She'd watched Dan last night and was pretty sure where to find things in the massive kitchen. Seemed everything about Dan was large. She grinned, thinking oh, how much that really was true.

The dogs huddled around her feet as she measured out the coffee. And when she turned to grab two mugs, she jumped and gasped. A middle-aged woman, dressed in black and wearing a white apron, entered the kitchen.

"Good morning," the woman said, giving Erin a pleasant smile.

She was obviously Dan's housekeeper. Oh Lord. Had she been in the house last night? Had she heard them going at it in the kitchen in the middle of the night? Heat rose up Erin's neck and her cheeks burned. "Hello. I'm, uh, Erin."

"Erin, glad to meet you. I'm Darla White. What would you like for breakfast? Dan always eats eggs, bacon and toast. If you'd like anything else, I'm happy to make it for you."

"Oh, no, thanks. Coffee is just fine. I, uh, got it started."

Mortified, Erin wanted to fall into a sinkhole.

The woman didn't take exception to her. She went about her business, pulling out frying pans, getting eggs out of the fridge. Was she used to having strange women show up in Dan's kitchen? Or was she just unusually tactful?

Dan walked into the kitchen then, his hair wet and combed back and the scent of freshly showered man and musky shampoo wafted in the air. He hadn't bothered to shave and the facial scruff today was darker, more pirate-like, sending chills up and down Erin's body. "Mornin'," he said.

Despite the effect he had on her, she wanted to bop him over the head for not warning her that aside from his menagerie, they hadn't been alone last night.

Dan scoped out the scene and arched a brow at Erin's state of embarrassment. "Darla, I'd like you to meet, Erin. Erin, this is Darla. She lives in the guesthouse on the property with her husband, Ted. Ted is foreman on the ranch."

Darla did her best to hide a smile, yet the silent communication going on between the two didn't fool her. And Dan's expression was bordering a grin. The rat. He'd known all along what she'd been thinking, but he'd also been quick to relieve her embarrassment.

Erin's cheeks began to cool as she sat quietly at the kitchen table while the housekeeper served the coffee. Dan walked over to the dog's bed in the corner of the room, crouched down and gave the animal a once-over. Lucky was already terribly in love. As Dan gave his head a pat, the dog scooted closer, licking Dan's hand, arm and face. Dan ate it up, displaying a killer smile. "Hey, boy, looks like you filled your belly a bit."

The water in his bowl was almost gone too. And when Dan straightened his body and stood, Lucky was right there, curling his body around his legs.

He shot Erin a quick look. "Excuse me. I've got to take him out to deal with nature."

"Of course."

Dan walked out the back door leading to a beautifully sculptured garden. Lucky had limped behind him to relieve himself in the tall grass and then follow Dan back inside the house. As he took his seat facing her, Lucky camped out beside Dan at the table. Maybe they should've named him Shadow.

Dan seemed totally at ease, while Erin was at a loss, wondering if they should discuss what had happened between them. She didn't know what to make of a one-night stand. She'd never done anything like this before. The few men she'd been with sexually she'd dated and had a relationship with. She'd never gone home with a guy she'd picked up in a bar.

Well, that wasn't exactly how it had happened with Dan. There were extenuating circumstances that had brought her to Dan's ranch. But that didn't diminish the fact they barely knew anything about each other. They'd had carnal sex last night, and emotions shouldn't get in the way. But Erin truly liked Dan. Sheesh, after last night, how could she not?

Darla served the food and then disappeared into another room of the house.

"Have some breakfast, Erin," Dan said. "You should eat."

"I'm not much of a breakfast person. Coffee and toast is fine."

She made a production of lathering butter on her

toast and then stared at it on her plate. Dan was so not a talker, so where did that leave her? She didn't want to be the cliché woman clinging to a man. She didn't want to ask, where did they go from here?

Dan sipped coffee and then cleared his throat. "I'll drive you to your car after breakfast."

"That's not necessary. I called a cab."

"Already?" He seemed truly surprised.

"Yes, a bit earlier this morning. The ranch is quite a ways out. I figured it might take a while for a taxi to get here."

Dan pursed his lips and leaned in, bracing his folded arms on the table. "I like you, Erin."

"I like you too, Dan."

"I, uh, don't want to be a jerk about this because last night was incredible, but I don't do long-term commitments and I don't think you're the kind of woman—"

"I get it. You don't have to say anything more." Oh man. He was about to hit her with the I'm-not-good-with-relationships speech. She didn't want to hear it. She knew the drill. But somehow she was gravely hurt and disappointed because, for her, last night had been about more than sex. It had been about relating to another human being. It had been about opening up and, yes, taking a risk. But Dan had laid down the rules. And she wasn't going to break a one of them. "Last night was amazing but that's where we'll leave it. Okay, Dan?"

He blinked a few times. For a second, he seemed uncertain and that was a small triumph.

"Yep," he said finally.

She took a bite of her toast and prayed the taxi wouldn't take too long to arrive.

Dan hated putting Erin in a cab. It seemed so impersonal. So doggone harsh. But she'd insisted and in the end, he'd thought maybe it was better that way. He gave her an awkward kiss and stood on the porch at Hunt Acres, surrounded by Rio, Buggy, Juliet and the rest, watching the yellow car drive off his property.

Once she was gone, he was struck by a deep sense of loss. Had he made a colossal mistake letting her go? Not even asking for her phone number.

"Fool," he said. She must think him an entitled rich bastard for sending her off that way. Hell, he would agree. Thirty-one years old and he was still pushing people away. Or rather, he pushed *women* away. He wasn't one to get caught up in a relationship that would eventually go awry. He liked his life the way it was. Risk-free. With no chance of getting injured. With no chance of being abandoned. Again.

Erin seemed different. Special. She was the first woman in a long time that he'd truly liked. It wasn't wise liking her so much. Dan was a loner and he wanted to keep his life simple. It was the standard he lived by these days. Don't get too close, don't allow anyone in. He kept his scars hidden, where they belonged. His dogs and cats filled the void that could otherwise consume him. And so he'd made up his mind after an incredible night together, that's where it had to end. He wasn't going to get involved with her. They'd met by chance, not by design.

Yet the look in her aquamarine eyes as she'd climbed into the back of that taxi popped into his head and hinted at disappointment and regret, hidden by a healthy dose of pride.

Dan strode into his study and sat at his desk. His computer counted some thirty-odd emails for him to go through. Hunt and Company, the family business that supplied beef to restaurants nationwide and ran its own chain of steak houses, chunked out a big portion of his life and he had a heavy workload to get through today. He opened the first email, narrowing his eyes, trying to make heads or tails of the message on the screen. The words didn't make a lick of sense because his mind was elsewhere.

"Is she gone?" Darla's voice broke into his scattered thoughts.

Grateful for the intrusion, he mentally thanked her for saving him from twenty-nine more daunting emails. Swiveling around in his chair, he faced his housekeeper. These days, she tended to keep more than his house, and some part of him appreciated that. "Yes. Erin is gone."

"You didn't drive her?"

Dan shook his head. "She was stubborn about it."

"She out-stubborned you?" Her voice reached a pitch of incredibility. It was not a compliment.

A chuckle rose from his throat, but with a hefty dose of guilt too. He hadn't fought Erin hard enough on that battle. "Yeah, guess so."

"Too bad. I liked her."

"You *liked* her?" Dan's brows gathered. "Is that some secret woman perception thing? You only just met her, how do you know you liked her?"

"Because, you liked her." She sighed and gave her head a shake. She was twenty years his senior and at times took to mothering him. "And let's face it, this house has been lacking female attention for a long time. Erin was very nice. She colored up redder than a greenhouse tomato when I walked into the room. That says something about a gal."

Dan noticed too and he'd tried to remedy her discomfort. "She helped me with the dog last night."

"I have no doubt." His housekeeper's smile was a little too bright.

"Hey Darla, give a guy a break, okay?"

She laughed. "I'm only saying you're gonna die an old lonely man if you don't step up your game."

"I don't have game."

"I'm beginning to think that's true, Dan. A pity."

She whirled out of the room as fast as she'd entered, and Dan turned back to his computer and stared at the screen. "Ah, hell." He was in no mood for work this morning.

He planted his feet, lifted from his seat and left the study, taking Darla White's words along with him.

Lucky's prognosis was good. Doc Bristol's exam determined the dog had no internal damage and Dan was given a dose of antibiotics to administer for a week. The dog should heal in time, with no residual problems. It was good news and Dan returned to the house by early afternoon.

He set to work in the study, reluctantly getting back to answering emails, checking over his accounts with the Cattleman's Club to make sure everything was set for the next few months of inventory. His company's steaks were a big draw at the club.

He forced himself to sit there until his work was done. Well, almost done. By four o'clock, he'd had enough of numbers and computer screens. He was restless, antsy. He didn't want to get into his head about why that was. He only knew he had to get outside.

The front door slammed shut behind him as he exited the house and fresh brisk November air hit him. He loved the fall, when the summer air cooled and the humidity vanished. Ah, a man could really breathe again. He stood on the veranda of the house, his sanctuary, and filled his lungs. He'd gotten used to the smells around him, until beeves and earth and leather all seemed to blend into one solid Hunt Acres scent. It tended to calm him down, to keep him leveled.

He strode down the stairs and followed the path to the corral. His mares, all three of them, trotted over as soon as they spotted him, hanging their heads over the top of the fence. "Hey, girls." He gave each one attention, stroking their manes and patting their shiny coats.

"How's your day going?" Ted asked, coming out of the stable, holding a handful of carrots.

"Hey, Ted. Fine. Just fine."

Ted handed him half the bunch of carrots and he gave two of his mares a treat, while Ted fed the other horse. All three mares chomped eagerly and waited for more.

"I hear you brought someone home with you last night."

Dan stilled. It wasn't anybody's damn business and it was uncanny how fiercely he wanted to protect Erin from any scrutiny. "You hear that from your wife?"

"Nope, not Darla. I saw the dog with my own eyes this mornin'. What happened this time, and is he stayin'?"

Dan choked back his relief. He should've known Ted would be more discreet. Even if he had seen Erin, he wouldn't have said anything. "Hit and run. I witnessed it and brought him to Doc Bristol. He's stayin' unless someone comes to claim him."

"Does the dog have a name?"

"Lucky."

"Fittin'. Him gettin' hit in front of you might've saved his life, that's for damn sure," Ted said, slapping him once on the back. "You never could resist a body in need."

Dan smiled at Ted's comment because it was so true.

And a little while later, he suited up in a pair of new denim jeans and a solid royal blue shirt. With his belly full thanks to Darla's fried chicken dinner, Dan gunned the engine in his four-wheel drive SUV and headed off the ranch. He knew where he was going and he told himself it was only to see if anyone at the Dark Horse was missing a half shepherd, half collie mix.

And once he arrived, he scanned the parking lot, finding clusters of people milling about by their cars, but no one looked familiar. No one was asking about a lost dog. A damn chuckle rose from his throat. He was such a fool. He'd blown it big-time and now was hoping to see Erin again. To find her, and then to do what? Hell, he didn't know.

He continued on until he was inside the saloon, standing at the bar. "Scotch. Double. Straight up," he told the bartender. The barkeep set a tumbler down in front of him and poured from a bottle two inches high. Dan took a healthy sip.

"Have you seen anybody come in here looking for their dog? Medium-sized collie-shepherd mix?" Dan asked the barkeep.

The guy shook his head. "Can't say as I have."

Just as well, Dan thought. He was growing fond of Lucky. He turned his back to the bar to look out into the crowded dance floor. A leggy brunette came out of nowhere and batted her eyes at him. She was put together, wearing a low-cut eye-popping blouse.

"Are you looking for your dog?" she asked.

"Something like that. I found a dog."

"Oh, um. Well, I can help you ask around if you'd like."

"No, thanks." He sipped his Scotch. "I'm good."

"I think so too," she said. Her eyes gleamed darkly, a flicker in them that would have most men paying the check and escorting her home. She leaned in closer. "I'm Yvonne."

Yep, ripe for the pickin', his buddies would say, but Dan wasn't interested.

"Yvonne, I was just about to call it a night. Thanks for the offer, but no thanks."

Her eyes snapped in surprise. "Sure," she said, her chin up as she pivoted on her three-inch heels and walked away.

Dan turned back to the bar and polished off his drink.

"Oh, man," the barkeep said.

Dan gave him a look. "What?"

"You're looking for that chick who rode the bull last night? You, uh, helped her out, right?"

Dan didn't respond.

The bartender shook his head. "She doesn't come in here. She's not a regular. Doubtful she'll be back. You can always tell, you know. This place didn't suit her, if you ask me."

"I didn't."

"There's always the internet. Look her up."

"What?"

The bartender grinned as if he knew all the truths in the world. What a dumbass. But Dan had to agree. Erin didn't fit in a place like the Dark Horse.

He was wasting his time. She wouldn't be back.

Three

"Thanks for inviting me to lunch, Chelsea," Erin said as she sat across from Chelsea Hunt in Royal's number one new resort, The Bellamy. "This place is amazing."

Erin didn't know Chelsea well, but she'd heard that Chelsea had been the latest of Maverick's victims. She'd been secretly photographed in the TCC locker room and those images had emerged on a popular internet site causing quite a splash. It had been a bold move on Maverick's part, to hack a hacker, Chelsea being the CTO of Hunt and Company. Her friendship with Max St. Cloud and Will Brady culminated in their being tasked to investigate the crimes. Erin's heart went out to Chelsea. It must have been so awful being violated like that.

"Yeah, I thought the two of us could use a break and I've heard The Glass House has incredible food."

The entire resort was something out of a modern tech dream and this restaurant, made of more windows than walls, looked out upon beautiful lush greenery mingled with colorful fall flowers. Inside the restaurant, everything from the napkin rings to the delicate chandeliers over each table was made of the finest handblown glass.

She and Chelsea had bonded one day over tall lemonades while playing with little Faye Brady on the Flying E Ranch. Erin missed her little eleven-month-old charge.

She was out of a job, too. With a ton of time on her hands and no prospects. Will had insisted on keeping her on his payroll until the end of the year and so she figured why not go to a five-star resort and splurge a little?

The little buggy voice in her head hollered, *Remember the last time you splurged?*

She'd splurged alright, on adventure at the Dark Horse Saloon and ended up having a one-night stand with a man that had topped her list as a forever kind of guy. A guy who took great care with animals. A man who didn't say much, but allowed his actions to speak volumes. A man who had treated her with the utmost respect.

Dan.

She sighed. It had been two weeks since their night together. And though she felt the loss of him all the way down to her bones, she didn't plan on splurging like that anytime soon. She'd stick to splurges like hot fudge sundaes at the Royal diner, or fifty-dollar lunches at a swanky resort.

Opening the menu, she glanced at all the choices. "Wow. I can't decide. It all sounds delish."

"If you like seafood, I recommend the scallops in lobster sauce."

The thought of it made her stomach clench. "I'm not really a fish person."

She was, sometimes, but today a meal doused in all that sauce didn't sound appealing. "I think I'll stick to something basic, like chicken."

They ordered their meals and sipped iced tea through colorful straws. While they were chatting, she caught Chelsea sighing and staring out the window a few times.

"And so the cat howled at the moon and the dog turned green."

Chelsea turned to face her, shaking off whatever it was in her head. "What? I'm sorry, I didn't hear you."

She smiled. "You went somewhere."

"Yeah, I did. Forgive me."

"It's okay. I think I know what it's about."

Chelsea stared into her eyes for a second and then shook her head. "I still can't believe some creep actually snapped nude photos of me in the club's locker room and posted them on *Skinterest* of all places. I'm no wilting willow, but I'm floored by his or her audacity. This Maverick has been causing havoc at

TCC for months now and we're no closer to finding out who it is than the day it all began."

Erin sympathized with her. She hadn't had nude photos displayed to the world, but she had been involved in a scandal in Seattle, and she knew how violated she'd felt when it all came down. She softened her voice. "Will shared some of that with me. Gosh, I'm so sorry. For a while, didn't they think they'd found the jerk doing this?"

"Yeah, there was some evidence pointing to Adam Haskell, even though the man hadn't any keen knowledge of computers, certainly not enough to cyber attack the residents of Royal. But it became obvious after Mr. Haskell died in a car crash that it wasn't him. Evidence had been planted in his car, making him a victim of Maverick too."

"Poor man."

"Yes, that's why I seem so distracted today. Those photos that surfaced are proof that the cyberbully is alive and well, and who knows what else he'll do."

"Chelsea, I've got nothing but time on my hands right now. I would love to pitch in and help in any way I can to help you find this guy. I'm not as tech oriented as you or Will, but I can come at it from a fresh perspective. Maybe find something hiding in plain sight."

"I think that's a great idea. I've been splitting my time between the investigation and working at the family business. I could really use the extra help. But are you sure?"

"Believe me, I'm sure. I know a little of what you're going through. That feeling of being betrayed and the helplessness that settles around your heart."

"Oh, wow, Erin. Sounds like you've had man trouble. Recently?"

Well, Chelsea was perceptive. And Erin wasn't going to hold back any longer. She didn't really have anyone here in Texas to talk to, and Chelsea had already shared so much with her. Fair was fair. Besides, Erin could use a friend and her inner voice was telling her she could trust Chelsea Hunt. "Yes, back in Seattle. It was an awful situation. I was involved with a man named Rex Talbot. Have you heard of him?"

"Vaguely, but I don't know much other than he runs a megacorporation. He keeps a low profile."

"Yes, well, when I met him, it was at a private school's music program. I'm a musical director and teacher by profession and initially I thought he was the father of one of the students. He was charming and lovely. My interest in him had nothing to do with money. It was the furthest thing from my mind, and I truly liked him. After our first date, he confessed that he was the school's anonymous benefactor. I was over the moon thinking I'd met such a kind and generous man. He told me he wasn't married and had no children and I had no reason not to believe him. He wasn't over-the-top, we did low-key things that didn't warrant any sort of glamorous news. I fell for him and we had an intimate relationship for months."

"And don't tell me, then his wife showed up?"

"Yes. Cliché, isn't it? I never thought it would happen to me. I was blinded by his charm and had no clue he was lying to me. But his wife, who had been out of the country the entire time, returned with a vengeance and found out about our relationship. As low-key as Rex was, his wife, a socialite from birth, made all kinds of noise in the local school district, thinking nothing about scandalizing my good name, blaming me, of course, for homewrecking. It was humiliating and the situation brought the school undue negative attention."

"Oh, wow. I'm so sorry, Erin."

"Thanks. But if there was a silver lining, it was that the school administration was wonderful, sticking up for me and defending my reputation. They asked me not to resign my position, but at that time, I was distraught and embarrassed for myself as well as the school. I appreciated their support more than they'll ever know, but I just couldn't stay on.

"The worst of it was that Rex didn't stick up for me. He crawled back to his wife and threw me under the proverbial bus. My judgment was way off and I made a big mistake."

"Honey, don't you dare put the blame on yourself. He lied to you. He led you on. He was a jerk. That's a fact."

A chuckle escaped her mouth and she grinned.

"You're right. I am so over Rex Talbot now. I figure the two of them deserve each other."

"For sure," Chelsea said. "I take it Will's job offer came at a good time for you?"

"It did. I needed change. Will's a good friend who went through a terrible loss when his wife died. We were both at loose ends, and so because he believed in me, he hired me as Faye's nanny. Oh, I loved taking care of that little doll. When Will's job brought him here to Royal, I came along as her nanny."

"Well, I'm glad you're here. I'm glad we've met. And if you're available to help with the investigation, I'm actually going to the club's main office tonight. My big brother was supposed to meet me, but something came up and he had to cancel. I plan on diving into some files. If you're free, you could help me. I know it's short notice and—"

"Of course. I would love to. What time?"

"Can you meet me at nine?"

"I'll be there."

That evening with a renewed sense of purpose, Erin entered the main entrance of the Texas Cattleman's Club, and showed her guest pass to the attendant at the front desk. It was late at night and the place, normally bustling with both men and *women*, now that the club allowed both sexes in equally, was nearly empty but for a few people walking out of the facility as she was walking in.

She strode past the dining area and secondary lobby, and walked down a long corridor of offices until she came to the door at the end of the hallway marked Texas Cattleman's Club and underneath, Staff Only.

She was ten minutes early and anxious to get started. She didn't mind the wait. This was the most exciting thing going on in her life since her ride on that bull and her encore ride—showing much more endurance with cowboy Dan—later that night.

She'd giggle and think it funny, but it wasn't a laughing matter. Not only did she miss the cowboy, not being able to get him off her mind, she'd also missed her period two days ago and she was normally right on schedule, month after month. Stress could mess up a woman's schedule, and it had only been two days, after all. She filled her lungs and steadied her breathing.

At least she could assist Chelsea in finding the sleaze who'd posted those pictures of her. Erin was glad she'd asked for her help. She'd been just about ready to throw in the towel and scurry back to her studio apartment in Seattle with her tail between her legs, as discouraging as that notion was.

On habit, she pulled out her cell and studied her phone messages, checking to see if Chelsea had texted. Then she heard the definite sound of footsteps on the floor, getting louder and heading her way.

She dumped her phone back into her purse and turned to face Chelsea.

Only, it wasn't Chelsea, it was a big tall handsome beast of a man, wearing a black Stetson, jeans and a tails-out white shirt. The sleeves were rolled up, hugging his biceps to distraction.

She blinked.

"Erin?"

The low timbre of his voice did crazy things to her, reminding her how he'd whispered her name over and over while making love to her.

"What are you doing here?" he asked.

His eyes were so blue, so amazingly bright right now, she wanted to throw her arms around him, but she also wanted to thrash his hide for not pursuing her, even a little.

"I'm, uh, meeting a friend," she said. "What are you...?" Then it dawned on her like some insanely wicked twist that maybe this wasn't a coincidence. Oh no. "You're not Chelsea's brother, are you?" she squeaked.

"You know my sister?"

Erin's eyes blinked shut. She couldn't believe this. She leaned her back against the door so it could hold her upright, rather than having her limbs crumble to the floor. She managed a nod.

"How?"

She opened her eyes. "We have mutual friends."

Dan moved in on her, his presence surrounding her like a fortress, his lime scent reaching her nostrils. He wasn't smiling, but his eyes blazed with some sort of relief. He put his hand up to touch her face, but then let his arm drop down before making contact. His gaze stayed on her and she didn't know which emotion to cling to, which emotion to believe: the one that wanted to invite Dan to touch her, because oh how she craved it; or the one that poured acid into her stomach, warning her not to go near him again.

"I went back to the Dark Horse the next night looking for you," he confessed.

"You don't have to say that."

"I say very little, but what I say means something." He spoke with enough authority to sway any nonbelievers.

She stared into his eyes, captivated by the honesty she saw in them. "Why?"

"Why?" He smiled then, an apologetic smile that touched something deep in her heart. "I wanted to see you again."

"Because?"

She wasn't letting him off the hook that easily. Even if she had to pry the words out of his mouth, she wanted to know what he was feeling.

"Because... Well, hell. I just did, Erin. We weren't through."

She gulped. "What does that mean?"

"I don't recall you asking me a ton of questions before."

"Yes, well...I never thought I'd see you again."

"Are you glad?"

"Are you?" she asked.

"Damn glad. I should've never let you go that morning. Not that way."

Those were words she'd been dying to hear. Words she never thought she would hear, because she didn't think she'd ever see Dan again. "Are you apologizing?"

"For the best night of my life? No. Can't apologize for that. Don't think you'd want me to, either."

Her face flushed from his blatant admission. Dan wasn't holding back. And somewhere deep inside she knew that this cowboy wasn't smooth or polished. But he was real. And he'd just paid her a compliment.

"I am sorry I didn't get your full name and number, Erin."

"Why didn't you?" After what they'd shared that night, she'd been baffled at his noncommittal attitude in the morning. She hadn't pegged Dan for a love-'em-and-leave-'em kind of man. Sure, Dan said he hadn't thought it smart for her to ride that bull, and then she'd blathered on and on about being from Seattle, losing her job and wanting to do something Texan. "Did you think I was a…" God she hated to say it. "A bimbo or something?"

Dan's smile only lifted half his mouth. "Exactly the opposite."

She shook her head. "I don't get it?"

The sound of footsteps rushing forward stopped Erin up short.

"I am *so* sorry I'm late." Chelsea reached the two of them at the door. She wore a fitted trench coat and an apologetic expression. "Erin, thanks for coming. I see you've met my brother Dan already. Good." Then she faced Dan. "Why are you here? I thought you weren't coming tonight, big guy. You had a date you couldn't get out of or something."

"I got out of it."

"You broke your date?"

Erin put her head down. This was awkward. Was that why Dan hadn't pursued her? He was dating someone. Her stomach squeezed at the slice of jealousy wedging tight inside.

"It wasn't a date, Chels," he said, slightly irritated. "You needed me, and I'm here."

"Thanks, bro. I appreciate it."

Then she turned and punched five numbers into the keypad on the wall and pressed a button. "Here we go." She opened the door before Dan could get to it and breezed into the room. Dan held the door for Erin and they followed inside, the door shutting closed behind them.

Erin immediately felt his big presence engulf them in the twelve-by-twelve room.

There were a few chairs and one good-sized desk in the middle of the room, while a dozen tall metal file cabinets lined three of the walls. The usual decor at the Cattleman's Club was spacious and generous with tall ceilings and an air of openness now, especially since the remodel after a tornado had swept through causing some destruction, but this out-of-the-way room reminded her of something she'd seen in an old detective movie, small, stuffy and dingy.

"This is where all the paper files are kept for the Cattleman's Club members," Chelsea said, removing her sleuthing coat. "Most records are digitally input now, but the club makes a habit of keeping all the original files. Some date back since the club's founding."

"So, what are we looking for exactly?" Dan asked, his brows doing that adorable bunching again.

Erin took a hard swallow and turned away, pretending interest in a file drawer labeled A-C. Dan hadn't mentioned that he knew Erin and she'd been too taken by surprise to correct Chelsea's assumption that they had never met each other. She was feeling guilty about that, but she couldn't very well blurt out now that she and Dan had hooked up for one wild night and then hadn't spoken again.

"Since all of Maverick's victims are members of the club, we've been given special permission to check into these files. The board and all the members don't like the negative publicity. It's hurting the club's reputation and we all want to catch the creep, sooner rather than later. We don't want him hurting anyone else, that's for sure.

"We're looking for anything that strikes you as odd. Something that would spark this guy's rage. Formal complaints registered against the club or a member. Anything that doesn't add up. Marriages, divorces, births. The computer files have been scoured already, but maybe something important didn't get input. We can't afford to skip over anything.

"The files reflect parties given at the club, including any violations or disturbances, tennis and golf lessons taken, holiday stuff. There's a lot to go through. And if we get anything substantial, we'll take what we find to the authorities to follow up on. I know it's a lot of work and I appreciate your help."

"Chels, you know I have your back," Dan said.

"I'm happy to lend a hand too, Chelsea."

"We're going to catch that asshole," Dan said forcefully.

Chelsea smiled. "I hope so. Either way, I appreciate you both for helping. Erin, my brother runs Hunt and Company, our family business and he also has a poor man's version of an animal rescue on his ranch at Hunt Acres. The man has a heart of gold and picks up strays faster than—"

Dan cleared his throat, loudly.

"Okay," Chelsea said, getting the hint. "My big bro is too humble. He doesn't like me expounding his virtues. So I won't. But, Dan, you should know that Erin is in between jobs right now," Chelsea seemed compelled to explain. "And she insisted on helping. She, well, she knows a little about what I've been going through from past experience."

Dan turned to look at Erin. One brow arched, his expression deeply curious. "Yeah?"

A cold shiver ran up and down her body.

Don't go there, Chelsea. I don't want to explain to Dan.

"None of your beeswax, big bro," she said, giving Erin a big smile, letting her know she wouldn't betray her.

Dan shot a mock frown at his sister. But Erin could see the determination in his eyes. He was ready to protect his sister, no matter what.

"Let's get down to business," Dan said.

"Sounds good," Chelsea said. "Dan, why don't you and Erin look at the files together? You can double-check each other, since we're not sure what we're fishing around for."

She turned to pull out the very same A-C drawer that Erin had focused on before. A stack of manila folders ten inches high landed on the desk in front of her. "Here you go."

Erin batted her eyes a few times and slowly lowered into a chair. Dan took the seat next to her at the desk, grinning at her behind Chelsea's back. She did a mental eye roll.

She was trapped in this tiny room with a man who made her pulse race.

"I'll take on the next batch," Chelsea said, reaching into the file cabinet again and didn't miss a beat, taking the chair opposite them and opening the first file in her huge stack.

Erin tried to concentrate on the words on the page. There were dates and information about spouses—very detailed records. In a way, she felt like a Peeping Tom, privy to strangers' lives, reading about things that were highly personal. Yet, she had to remember that somewhere in these files they could find clues to Maverick. Chelsea's ordeal made it more personal for her, as a woman. No one had the right to violate a woman's privacy that way. No one had a right to secretly stow away to take nude photos and then publicly humiliate someone.

Just thinking about it, ticked her off all over again.

"It just isn't fair," she whispered.

Dan's head snapped up. She couldn't believe she just blurted that out. "If I catch the guy—" he started to say.

"Dan," Chelsea said. "Thank you, big brother. But I don't want you getting thrown into jail for assault."

"More like murder." A tick worked at Dan's jaw and the set of his chin made him look dangerous.

"Dan!"

He shook his head. "Kiddin'."

He gave Erin a quick glance and winked. She'd bet her entire bank account, tiny as it was, that although Dan would love to give the jerk more than a piece of his mind, he wouldn't resort to any sort of violence.

"You better be kidding," Chelsea said, "and believe me, I appreciate the support."

After going over dozens of files, Erin's eyeballs burned and she glanced at her watch. It was almost midnight and immediately as if her body clock was rebelling, she yawned. Chelsea caught her in the act and yawned, as well. "You know what? We should call it a night. Dan gets up at dawn and it's later than I realized."

They'd made a bit of progress, piling up a stack of member files that they could rule out. The initial process of elimination was a good start, but it wasn't near enough.

"I can come back again anytime," Erin offered. She liked being a part of something and having a purpose again.

"Count me in too," Dan said.

Of course Dan wanted to help, but didn't he have a big mega ranch to run? It baffled her how she hadn't put two and two together when she'd first met Dan. Hunt Acres. Hunt, as in Chelsea Hunt. Hello.

"That's great," Chelsea was saying, "but I have that darn convention in Houston tomorrow. I'll be gone for a few days. Unless," she said, narrowing her eyes at her brother, "you step in for me and represent the ranch."

Dan shook his head. "Not a chance in hell," he said. "I'm no good at that stuff."

"Kidding," Chelsea said. "But that means we can't get together again until the weekend."

"Give me the key code to this room, Chels. I'll come back as often as it takes."

"Really?"

"Yeah."

"I shouldn't. But you are a long-standing member and you'd be under my authority," she teased.

Dan snorted, and the sound echoed in the boxy room.

Erin giggled, a nervous little laugh that she sometimes couldn't control. Both sets of eyes turned her way. She gulped air. In for a penny, in for a freaking pound. "I'm available too."

She couldn't look Dan in the eye after that comment, yet she sensed his gaze piercing her. All that blue heading her way could make a girl dizzy, so she ignored him and nodded to Chelsea. "There's a lot to still go through."

"True. Thank you. I'll leave the details to Dan and you can work it out with him. If that's okay?"

"It's…fine," she said, finally looking at him and relaying in unspoken words that this didn't mean anything. She would work alongside him to help Chelsea with her investigation. Period.

"Fine by me too," he said in a clipped tone.

And then gave her a solid look that said something much different.

After saying good-night to Chelsea, Erin headed across the parking lot toward her car. Dan walked beside her, and no amount of arguing could convince him he didn't need to escort her. The parking lot was lit like the Fourth of July, but Dan wouldn't take no for an answer and rather than make a scene in front of Chelsea, she shrugged her shoulders, aware of the big man slowing his strides to keep pace with her shorter steps.

"It's a good thing you're doing, helping my sis," he said, breaking the ice. But with Dan it wasn't idle small talk. Dan meant it. She could give him that. He was loyal to his sister and obviously loved her very much.

"It was horrible, what Chelsea went through. I'm happy to do what I can."

"She appreciates it. And so do I."

They took a few more steps together before Erin asked, "How's Lucky?"

The dog had been on her mind lately and she couldn't very well ask Dan about him while they were in the office with Chelsea. Caught off guard and with bad timing, neither one of them had volunteered to Chelsea that Erin and Dan had already met. Looking back on it, it was a mistake. They could've made something up quickly to keep the deception to a minimum. Erin liked Chelsea too much to hide the truth from her, but it was sort of too late now.

"He's doin' well," Dan said.

"That's good to hear. He's such a sweet boy. I've been thinking about him a lot. Are you keeping him?"

"Unless someone comes to claim him. I've put out word."

Erin kept on walking. Only ten more feet until she reached the little Toyota that Clay Everett had generously provided to let her drive while staying in Texas. Not only had he and Sophie put a roof over her head in an adorable cabin in their ranch, they'd given her wheels too. The Everetts had been gracious hosts to Will and now to her too. They'd taken southern generosity to a whole new level.

When they reached her car, she finally gazed up at Dan. "Well, this is me. Thanks for walking me."

A small acknowledging grunt pulled from his

throat. There was more in his eyes, something he wanted to say, but until he made up his mind to say it, wild horses couldn't drag it out of him.

"Good night," she said, turning to unlock the door.

"Erin." The way he ground out her name and the slightly desperate tone of his voice had her turning back around.

"Yes?"

"I'm no good with—"

"I get it, Dan. You're forgiven for whatever you think you need to explain to me. You and I had one night. It was pretty terrific," she said, granting him a small smile. For a minute there, she thought he was going to say something different, something she secretly wanted to hear. "But it ended and—"

He cut her off by stepping close and cupping her face in his hands. Taken by surprise, she sucked in oxygen and the next thing she knew, Dan's lips were all over hers, firm and demanding and oh wow, almost desperate. She didn't even try to stop him. It would be futile. He was a man of action, not words, and right now he was telling her things she wanted to hear.

He was sorry he hadn't called her.

He really liked her.

He didn't want this to end.

She heard all that in his kiss. In the way he pressed her body up against the car and roped his arms around her shoulders, closing the gap between them as he moved in. She heard it in the relieved breath he took between kisses and the small but convincing things he was revealing to her. "I'm no good with words, sweetness," he whispered. "That's what I wanted to say."

As his kisses deepened, she broke out in goose bumps, her entire body standing on end. It was the same ridiculous magnetic pull they'd had the other night.

When she couldn't stand it another second, little tiny whimpers rose from her throat. Those sounds hopefully relayed to him that she understood, that she wanted more also, that she really liked him too. Because she couldn't say those words aloud yet. She couldn't trust in what she was feeling. But she wanted to, and that was progress against Rex's ultimate betrayal and the scars he'd left her with.

It was obvious they had something going. Maybe it was simply lust. Maybe it was real chemistry. But maybe it was something more. They could barely keep their hands off each other. Here they were in a deserted parking lot, kissing like two teenagers who had snuck out without their parents' permission.

She was taken by surprise when Dan broke off the kiss, took hold of her shoulders, gave a squeeze and backed away from her. She already missed the comfort of his body, felt the cool midnight November air hit her like a pack of ice.

"I think we should call it a night," he said on a big sigh. "Get a little breathing room."

She blinked. Was he backing off again? What kind of game was he playing with her, kissing like his life depended on it and then shutting her down? Her engines were running hot and she was ready to unleash her fury.

Then Dan spoke again. "I want two things. To find whoever did this vile thing to my sis, and to get to know you better. I don't want to meet you in some stuffy office tomorrow night."

"What do you want?" she asked, truly curious and not sure where he was going with this.

"Dinner, with you. And then work at either my place or yours. Are you interested?"

"Dinner, as in a date?"

He nodded.

"Are you asking me out?"

Amused, he smiled. "What's your last name?"

"Sinclair."

"Erin Sinclair," he said, as if tasting her name on his lips. "Yes, I am asking you out on a date. Would you like to have dinner with me?"

"Well, now that you put it that way, Dan Hunt. Yes I would."

His next smile was of relief. "Thank you."

"And work at my place, afterward," she added.

She wanted to be on her own turf, in case things went sour. She wasn't sure where Dan's head was at, but she had a feeling their kiss tonight was as good an indicator as she was going to get from him. "But how will you get the files?"

"I have the pass code and permission, remember? I'll double back and grab the next batch of files and we'll look them over after we have dinner."

"Are you sure?"

"You might not know this about me, but I eat dinner all…the…time." He grinned.

She laughed, her mood lightening up considerably. Dan had a sense of humor, after all. And she wondered what a real date with Dan Hunt would be like.

Four

Sunlight cut through the white shutters cracked slightly open in Erin's bedroom, lending brightness without any real heat. The morning air brisk and cool, she cuddled down into her covers, her head cushioned by a fluffy pillow. Her guest quarters at the Flying E Ranch were like a dream. More cottage than ranch cabin, she was surrounded by a picturesque garden that kept on giving, regardless of season, thanks in part to the groundskeeper, who always had a smile and wave for her.

Tapestries covered the walls in flowery settings, and she focused her gaze on one of them. But the artwork, a cobblestone path leading to a birdbath pond, soon obscured in her mind as an image of Dan entered, popping into her head, just like that.

She smiled. Her discovery that he was Chelsea Hunt's brother had shocked her, but seeing her hadn't shocked Dan. He'd seemed glad, although she shouldn't make too much of his apparent relief at seeing her again. Because, according to her latest tally, most men didn't live up to the hype, *and* their meeting again had been purely accidental.

Yet, it had been torture sitting beside Dan during the night, trying to concentrate on files when her mind was going to the secret places Dan had taken her. And then, before she could escape the parking lot unscathed, he'd kissed her, landing a knockout blow that had left her shaking.

Suddenly restless, Erin tossed off her covers and sat up in bed. She had a date with Dan tonight. She hadn't been on a date since Rex. But he no longer counted. She was removing him from any importance in her life. The floor felt cool to her feet as she rose and padded over to her closet. It wasn't what she'd call brimming with clothes, she'd left much of her stuff back in Seattle, but after a quick scan, she gave her head a bob. She could work with what she had and put together an outfit for her date tonight.

That settled, she slipped on her robe and ambled into the kitchen to set a pot of coffee to brew. She had approximately ten hours before Dan would pick her up for dinner and she created a schedule to keep herself busy. She'd take her daily jog around the ranch, tidy up the cottage, bake a cake, and continue her job search for a position back in Seattle.

Her present situation ended on December 31. After that, she'd have to head home, jobless.

Working on the investigation made her feel useful. She looked forward to solving the mystery of Maverick or at least, lending a hand in tracking the cyberbully down. From what she'd gathered, he'd attacked one member of TCC after another over the months and it was why Will Brady, her ex-employer, had been called to Royal in the first place.

After a breakfast of raisin toast and coffee, she dressed in a pair of faded comfy workout pants and a deep purple sweatshirt marked by the Washington Huskies logo, and went outside. She jogged the ranch grounds stretching her legs and breathing in the crisp cool air. It was warmer than winters in Seattle, and there was sunshine, something you didn't see in Seattle too often.

Half an hour later, she had her hand on the cabin doorknob, ready to head inside and face her computer, when a familiar voice rang out. "Morning, Erin. Wait up."

She turned to find Will Brady coming up the path, holding little Faye in his arms. The little one recognized her and bounced in her daddy's arms. Erin's heart melted. "Will, good morning to you too."

When Will reached her, Faye was holding her arms out and Erin immediately grabbed her. "Hello, my little princess. How are you this morning?" Every time she spoke to Faye, her voice rose an octave and today was no different. She gave Faye a big fat kiss on her rosy cheek and set her on her hip. It was as natural as breathing, holding this baby.

"I hope we're not disturbing you. Are you busy?" Will asked.

"Yes, I'm busy holding your adorable little girl, and offering you a cup of coffee. Come inside."

Will laughed and entered the house behind her. "Have a seat," she said. Using her free hand to open the pantry door, she pulled out a box of teething crackers, leftover from when she was Faye's nanny. "Can she have one?"

The baby spotted the box and was reaching for it.

"Of course," Will said.

Erin handed Faye a cracker and the baby immediately went to town on it.

"Sit. I'll pour you a cup of coffee," she said. She knew how Will liked his coffee, black with two spoonfuls of sugar.

"No, thanks, Erin. But I'll sit with you."

He pulled out a chair for her and she took a seat, planting Faye comfortably on her lap. "How are you?" she asked.

"We're all great." It did Erin's heart good seeing how happy Will was now. He'd been closed off before, a widower grieving the loss of his wife, and now that he'd found love with Amberley, vibrancy had come back into his life.

"Wonderful."

"How are you, Erin?"

"Me? I'm doing fine. Enjoying my time here."

Will glanced at the papers she had strewn about

the other end of the long table, along with her computer ready to be fired up. "I have good news. At least I hope you'll think it's good news for you."

Erin flashed him a look. "For me? What kind of news?"

"A job in Seattle. How would you like to interview for a full-time music teacher position? It's at a private elementary school in Seattle."

"Really? That would be perfect. I've been doing a job search every day and I haven't seen this come up."

"I know a guy who knows a guy," Will said.

"You pulled some strings for me?" Erin was touched.

"You helped me raise Faye, Erin. I trusted you with my child and you did a great job. So, I owe you. Besides, it's not all that nefarious. My friend told me the music teacher at his school is going to have a baby. She's working until the end of the year and then plans on being a stay-at-home mom afterward. I simply put in a few good words for you."

"Thank you."

Will nodded. "They will set up a phone interview soon. The rest is up to you. And you can stay on here through the holidays. There's no rush to go back to Seattle. We want you to have Thanksgiving with us."

"Oh, uh…this is good news. I've been trying to figure out where to go from here. Your faith in me means a lot."

"Do you need time to think it over?"

She gave her head a shake. "I don't think so.

It seems perfect. I need a job and you know I've wanted to get back to teaching kids about music." She came partly out of her chair, baby and all, to give Will a kiss on the cheek. "Thanks again for the opportunity. I don't know what else to say."

"Say you'll always be in our lives. I want Faye to know you too."

"Of course. You won't be able to get rid of me. We'll always stay friends."

"Yep," he said. "I have no doubt."

"And now," she said, giving Faye her full attention, "my little princess is about to meet the tickle monster."

Erin carried Faye to the sofa and the baby gave her a five-toothed grin, knowing exactly what was to come. She tickled Faye under her chin, a sensitive spot that never failed, and the giggles began. They were the softest, sweetest sounds Erin had ever heard. One day she hoped to have a child of her own as sweet and adorable as Faye.

And that day may come sooner than she expected. She was still late.

And she didn't want to start thinking about what that could mean.

Dan knocked on Erin's door at precisely six o'clock. Erin opened it and her eyes immediately flew to the yellow roses he held in his hands. Her mouth gaped a little and she gave her pretty head a tilt. He didn't date much, but he knew how to treat a lady. The pleased look she granted him was well worth his effort. He loved how her eyes brightened when something made her happy.

"Hello, Dan." Her voice was sultry, soft, inviting. A force of nature couldn't hold back his smile at that greeting. "Come in."

He stepped inside and offered up the roses, his fingers brushing over hers gently, igniting a spark that traveled the length of him. "For you."

"Thank you." She admired the roses and hugged them to her chest. "They're lovely."

"So are you," he said, without skipping a beat. Erin looked dazzling tonight in a pretty sky blue dress that heightened the unusual aqua hue in her eyes and allowed a view of creamy shoulders and nice legs. The dress fit her form, showing off her tiny waist and shapely curves.

Dan removed his Stetson and kept it pressed to his side.

"Thank you again," she said. "Would you like a drink before we go?"

"Hold that thought until later," he said.

Her chin rose in question. "We'll need coffee to keep us awake. I've got a huge stack of files to go over after dinner. But first, I must feed you."

Erin laughed. "Let me get my jacket," she said. "I'll just be a sec."

While she was out of the room, Dan sauntered around the cabin, making note of her view out the parlor window, the stone fireplace and the homey feel of the place. Entering the kitchen area, the only thing not tidied up was a small mound of papers left out at the edge of the table beside her computer. He walked over and gave it a glance, scanning the top paper for a second, feeling guilty for doing so, but curious enough not to let that stop him. Apparently she was looking for work as a music teacher. In Seattle.

The thought of Erin leaving town left him with two thoughts. One was relief, because he knew her departure would guarantee nothing of permanence between them and that steadied his nerves some. His mother's abandonment when he was a kid had never really healed. He'd been injured more than anyone would ever know because Dan didn't show his feelings. He didn't talk about them. He only felt them, down to his bones. As a boy, he'd learned to hide his emotions from his dad, his sister, Chelsea, and his brother, Bradley. They'd been raised motherless by a father so heartsick over losing the woman he loved, he'd died early in life. Dan's mother was out there somewhere, but she'd never contacted the family again. It was as if they didn't exist.

Erin was leaving town. But Erin Sinclair was also getting under his skin. Quickly. He'd had no intention of asking her on a date, yet here he was, like a lovesick pup, waiting for her to enter the room so his heart could turn those somersaults again.

Dan was back in the parlor when Erin returned. "I'm ready," she said, wearing a pretty waist-length leather jacket over her dress.

Looking at her vanquished the darkness inside him and he lit up again.

* * *

Erin sipped Pinot Noir in a cozy corner booth of a restaurant called The Oak House. Dark wood beams above caught the flicker of candlelight from an array of twinkling votives placed around the room. Their table was topped with a textured cream tablecloth and a bowl of deep red roses. Across the room a live band played soft music on a stage and a few couples sashayed to country music on the polished wooden dance floor.

Dan sat next to her, looking over the menu, giving her time to study his profile, the deep angles on his face, the contours defining his masculinity and the scruff on his jaw that always cast him in a dangerously sexy light. His hair curled at the bottom of his collar and she wanted to wrap her fingers around them and give them a hard tug.

She giggled.

Dan's eyes snapped. "What?"

"Nothing. I'm just thinking."

He stared at her with those blue eyes. Over the flicker of the candles his gaze was mesmerizing. "Of?"

"You don't want to know."

"Maybe I do." He gave her a killer smile.

"On second thought, I don't want to tell you. But it's a good thing."

He closed the menu and set it down, giving her his full attention. "A good thing, huh?"

Then he turned to her and gave her a perfect kiss on the mouth. Enough to shock her, but not enough to cause a scene in the fancy restaurant. "That's what I was thinking."

"I didn't ask."

"Imagine what you'd get if you did."

Her eyes opened wider, the comment suggestive enough to make her melt. Heat burned her cheeks and she blushed. As if that wasn't embarrassing enough, she let out a tiny gasp.

Dan grinned, very happy with himself, and took a sip of wine.

She buried her face in the menu, her momentary hideout, until the color faded from her cheeks.

"See anything you like?" he asked.

She put down the menu and met his eyes. "I see a few things I'd like to set my fork into."

He laughed wholeheartedly and so did she. Then he rose from his chair and offered his hand. "Dance with me."

This she didn't expect. She didn't peg Dan for a dancer. But then, Dan did express himself more with actions than words. Oh boy, did he. She didn't make him wait. She placed her hand in his, and as he closed over her fingers, a sensation spread across her body like warm honey. She followed him to the middle of the room.

The band played a sweet country ballad, the lead singer crooning mellow lyrics and the soft sounds drifted to her ears. Dan took hold of her waist and she set her hands on his shoulders. Underneath her fingertips she felt his strength and power, but as he began to move, she marveled at how graceful he was. "You're a good dancer," she said.

"Surprised?"

"A little."

He nodded his head, a smile curving his lips.

"When did you learn?"

"A while back."

"That's not really an answer, Dan," she said softly. The more time she spent with him, the more he intrigued her. And the more she wanted to learn about him. But he wasn't a man who spoke more than he had to and yet she continued to press. "I would love to know how you came to dance so beautifully."

"Beautifully? No one's ever said that to me before."

He moved her around the dance floor, gliding easily and she gazed up at him, waiting.

"My best friend's mom taught me."

"What?" she blurted.

He grinned at her reaction. "That's why I don't tell people."

"Please, tell me. I want to hear this."

He debated a few seconds. "I was big and clumsy in high school, towering over everybody. Couldn't get a date to save my life."

She found that hard to believe, but didn't question him. She didn't want to distract him from telling this story.

"Peter's mom had been a professional dancer before she came to live in Texas. She overheard me complaining about how clumsy I was. I mean to say, she could see it with her own eyes. It wasn't a huge revelation that I was a clod, I tripped over my own feet daily. At that rate, I'd never get a girl to date me, much less go to the prom. I think she took pity on me."

"So she offered to teach you how to dance?"

"She did. Mrs. Brewer was very kind. She told me, once I felt confident on the dance floor, I wouldn't be so clumsy at school and that would solve two problems. At first, I declined her offer. I mean, it seemed so weird and all. But Peter egged me on and I finally agreed."

"Wow, well you can tell her she did a fine job."

"I think she knows."

"So what happened to Peter and his mom?"

"Peter is a colonel in the army. He comes home from time to time."

"And his mom? Does she still live here?"

"She does. She runs a dance studio for underprivileged children."

"Really? That's wonderful. What's it called?"

"I don't recall, actually," he said, with a shake of his head.

And then she was pulled close, so that Dan's big body brushed intimately with hers and she could feel his heat. Her arms automatically roped around his neck and she laid her head on his chest. Rapid beats of his heart pulsed in her ear. "Dan?"

"Hmm?"

"Mrs. Brewer's place, it isn't called Dan-cing Dreams, is it?"

He didn't say a word.

"I remember passing it in Royal. I thought it odd, the way it was spelled. She named it after you, didn't she?"

Silence.

And then she knew, as sure as she knew her own name. "You had something to do with financing the studio, didn't you? I bet you gave Mrs. Brewer a place to teach dance."

She moved her head off his chest to look up at him. But his eyes rested somewhere over her head, refusing to connect with hers. "I'm right, aren't I?"

"You talk too much, sweetness. Anybody ever tell you that?" Then he cupped the back of her head, guiding it back to his chest and began taking long sweeping strides across the dance floor that required her utmost concentration to keep pace.

Which quite effectively shut her up.

"My folks live in a retirement village in Arizona," Erin said to Dan. She was taking the finishing bites of her quinoa salad. Dan had arched a brow when she'd ordered butternut soup and salad for dinner. The place was known for their cuisine he'd told her, but he didn't press the issue at her simple meal. Instead, he'd asked her about her life. And she'd started in the easiest place, telling him about her parents. "They're blissfully happy and lead a very active life there."

He nodded, polishing off a tenderloin steak. Of course. Dan was a cattleman. He was probably a connoisseur and knew what a good steak should taste like.

"We're close, in that we talk all the time. And we try to make time to see each other. But they're gone a lot. They travel with a group and love every minute of it. They've earned it. They worked hard all their lives."

"What did they do for a living?" he asked, seeming genuinely interested. As far as dates went, this one rose above all her others. Dan was attentive, mannerly, sweet, funny and humble. He'd seemed to get truly disconcerted when she'd guessed, by her skills of brilliant deduction, that he'd built that dance studio for his friend's mother. Clearly, he didn't want to talk about it. He didn't want to take credit for doing something so incredibly generous.

Finally, she'd met a man with integrity.

"Dad was an attorney for most of the thirty-five years they've been married. My mom worked as a school administrator. After I came along, Mom took a few years off, but went right back to work as soon as I was in school full-time. They were both workaholics and now, I have to say, they're playaholics."

Dan chuckled at her made-up word. He was doing a lot of smiling tonight. It looked good on him. As if the man needed anything else in his favor, now he was granting her luscious smiles.

"And what about you?" he asked. "Have you always been a nanny?"

"Not at all. I'm a music teacher by profession. I learned how to play piano early on. I took to it naturally, according to one of my instructors, and I really did love it. If asked to practice for half an hour every day, I'd practice for an hour or longer. It kind of shocked my folks, pleasantly, I should say. They encouraged my love of music and it's always been a part of my life in one way or another. I would sing in live productions in high school and college. Sometimes, I'd accompany the orchestra. I haven't a clue where my musical abilities come from, really, since my folks both are analytical."

"I would love to hear you play some time," he said.

"Me? It's been a while." She shrugged. "I'm afraid I'm rusty. Haven't played for a while."

"But you play when you teach school, right?"

"I did. But I, um… I had to resign my last teaching position." She didn't want to discuss Rex. First dates, even if they were doing this all backward since they'd already broken the ice *in bed*, shouldn't involve talk of your past heartaches.

Dan's brow furrowed and before he could ask about her resignation, she quickly moved on. "I was lucky enough to land the position of nanny for little Faye Brady, back in Seattle. She was motherless and poor Will had his hands full. I love kids, and he needed a nanny, so it all worked out for those months

I took care of Faye." She heard her voice softening. "She's a little sweetheart."

Dan's gaze flicked over her, blinking rapidly as if he'd just learned something else new about her. "I hope to meet her one day."

"I hope you do."

The conversation died then and the silence was sort of nice. As far as she was concerned, she could stare into his blue eyes all night. But then the real reason for this date popped into her mind. To feed her before they dove into the investigation again.

They'd had drinks, danced, eaten and now she was gawking at him which was pretty darn unsettling because Dan was gawking back. "We should probably get to those files," she whispered.

Dan's forehead crinkled, as if he too had lost sight of their main purpose tonight. "Would you like to have dessert before we go?"

"Dessert is waiting at my house. It's a surprise." She gathered up her jacket and purse. "You won't be disappointed."

Dan cleared his throat. "You're full of surprises, sweetness."

As soon as they arrived at her cottage, Erin set out the coffeemaker and reached into the cupboard for a pair of rose-patterned china coffee cups rimmed in gold that matched the dessert plates. The cabin came equipped. There was nothing she found lacking when she'd set about creating her grandmother's recipe. The dessert was a family favorite and it was waiting in the refrigerator to make a grand entrance. But they'd both agreed to let the dinner settle a bit before indulging.

Dan set out the TCC files on the table and began flipping through one folder. Deeply engrossed in his work, his head didn't come up once as he scoured over the pages. She sat down next to him, grabbed a file and immersed herself in the papers.

They'd just had a great dinner date and learned some things about each other. Well, Dan had learned about her life, since he'd asked and she'd answered. But Dan didn't seem to like answering questions about himself and she'd had to pry and guess her way through some of the conversation tonight. Even with that, it was one of the best dates of her life. Mainly because Dan was a what-you-see-is-what-you-get kind of man. How refreshing. He didn't mince words and didn't try to charm her. But his charm came through anyway.

She half feared that they wouldn't get any work done tonight, repeating the last time she'd been alone with Dan. Hot kisses, soft caresses and then mind-blowing sex. But to his credit, and hers, if she was being honest, they'd gotten down to work immediately, both wanting to help Chelsea more than give in to temptation.

A while later, Dan's chair scraped back and he got up and walked over to the coffeemaker. Holy crap, she'd forgotten about the coffee.

"Sorry, Dan. I got lost in this file," she said, standing up.

"Sit," he ordered her pleasantly. "I can serve you a cup of coffee. Black with one sugar, right?"

He remembered. "Yes. Uh, thanks." She sank down into her seat and watched Dan move around in the kitchen.

"No problem. You finding anything worthwhile?" he asked.

"No, are you?"

"Nothing yet. Nothing even close." Dan let go a frustrated sigh as he set the delicate cup down in front of her and took his seat again. "This may be a big waste of time," he mumbled.

"I hope not. There's got to be something in these files that might point to Maverick."

Dan ran his hand down his jaw. "The thought of that guy getting away with what he did to Chels doesn't sit right with me."

"I agree." She shrugged and gave him a sympathetic smile.

His eyes flickered for a second and he leaned over her chair and touched his mouth to her cheek, pressing a kiss there. Then he took his seat, cleared his throat, avoiding her gaze, and opened a new folder.

She did the same, putting her head down to concentrate on a file. Every so often, she would lift her head to stretch the kinks out of her neck or sip coffee and their eyes would meet.

A flash of something hot would stream through

her body and she'd force her head down to peer at the file again. They were fully aware of each other, an electric spark that ignited with every glance, stolen or otherwise. Dan, in his dark slacks and blue button-down shirt he nearly muscled out of, looked good enough to eat.

Then she remembered. "Dessert," she blurted.

"What?" His head was just coming out of the file.

"I promised you dessert and it's almost midnight. I'm so sorry."

He turned his wrist to look at his watch. "It's a little after eleven. And there's no rule that says we can't indulge in a midnight snack. Is there?"

"No, of course not."

"I'm game. If you are." He patted his flat stomach and her gaze flew there, remembering what that taut skin felt like under her palms. Remembering too many things about being naked with Dan.

"Let me get it," she said, retrieving the pretty plates and putting them on the table while Dan pushed aside the folders.

"Need help?"

She shook her head. "I'm good."

She brought out the cake plate and placed her rather beautiful creation in front of him. This time, thank goodness, the cake had come out perfect. She'd had her share of mishaps over the years, but she'd taken more time and care and made a big deal about getting everything just right. For Dan. "Have you ever had hummingbird cake?"

He eyed the tall two-layer tower covered in buttercream frosting and chopped pecans. "Wow. Nope. I think I'd remember if I had. What's inside?"

She smiled, relieved and it unnerved her how much she wanted to please this man. "Cake."

His brows lifted and the next thing she knew her hand was snatched and she was tugged down. She landed with a plop onto Dan's lap. "Don't be cute," he said. Then he thought about it and said, "Never mind, you can't help it."

"I'm *cute*?"

Dan nodded, not giving her anything else to go on.

Was it a good thing that a gorgeous man with whom she'd had earth pounding sex just called her cute? Shouldn't he be saying she was alluring, tempting, stunning? Okay, not stunning, but maybe something along those lines.

Sitting on his lap this way, she peered down into his eyes. They were smiling, so blue and clear.

"Bananas and pineapple and stuff…is inside the cake."

Dan did that adorable thing with his brows and shook his head.

"It's my grandmother's recipe and not all that easy to make, I might add, so I hope you enjoy it. I mean, it's really good but it's not everyone's cup of tea, not that you drink tea, b—"

"Erin?"

"What?"

His hand splayed the back of her head and she caught sight of the ceiling tiles as she was lowered down in his arms. His eyes reached hers first, and then his mouth came dangerously close to hers, speeding up her heartbeat. "You went to a lot of trouble for me," he rasped. "I appreciate it." Then his mouth was on hers, tasting her, licking at her, as if she was the dessert. As if he couldn't get enough.

Dan had her at his mercy. She was in a vulnerable position, lying across him this way, his strength and power evident in the way he held her in his lap. He could easily shed her clothes, touch her until touching wasn't enough, and she would let him and relish every single second. But as soon as that thought struck, her world was upended again, literally. Dan brought her up quickly to a sitting position.

He brushed a kiss to her mouth, tightened his hold on her and gave her a wobbly smile. "Feed me cake."

She blinked and then a chuckle broke from her chest. "From here?" From her perch on his lap?

He nodded. "Do it, Erin. I'm having trouble being a gentleman here."

He didn't need to be a gentleman. Not after that display. He could've taken her right on the kitchen table and he had to know that, but there was a look in his eyes, and a tone to his voice that didn't warrant an argument. "Okay," she whispered softly.

She turned slightly to pick up the knife. The piece she cut separated nicely and the cake was firm and moist as she carefully held it and swiveled her body back to him. Their eyes met then, his gleaming in anticipation, and she knew then that Dan was wrecking her from enjoying cake in the customary way, ever again. His mouth opened and she pushed the frosting-topped cake into his mouth.

He chewed and groaned and his eyes shuttered closed. "Real good. Too good for me not to share," he said, reaching out for another piece. He offered it to her and slowly, keeping her eyes trained on his, she opened her mouth. Sugary banana scents wafted to her nose, just as Dan guided the piece inside.

"Mmm," she muttered and chewed. Just the right texture, just the right taste.

She fed him and he fed her and it was like something out of an erotic fairytale, without the sex. It was wildly arousing sitting on Dan's lap, feeding him a lush dessert by hand.

Dan was equally aroused; he had no hope of hiding it with her on his lap. Her breaths grew heavy and her heartbeat raced, and just when she thought this night wasn't going to end with cake, Dan lifted her off him, stood up and brushed crumbs from his shirt. "Thank you," he said. "It was delicious."

She stood facing him, wondering what the heck was going on. Dan brought that curious notion out in her more than she'd like to admit. "I'm glad you enjoyed it," she said more harshly than she intended.

"I, uh, it's late. I should go." His face contorted a bit, as if he couldn't believe he'd just said that. She could gain some comfort in knowing it wasn't easy for him to leave.

"Okay." What else could she say? *I wish you wouldn't go.* "Thank you for dinner."

"Thank you for dessert. I don't think I'll... Never mind."

"What?" Anger bubbled up. "Can't you finish a thought?"

"Hell, yeah, I can finish a thought," he barked back.

"Then just say it, Dan. Say what you want to say and be done with it." Her voice rose way above her normal pitch.

"Okay, I'll say it, damn it. It was the best first date I've ever been on. I don't want to leave, but I'm going, because I want to take you out again. I don't want you to think I'm just here to—"

God, the man of few words was giving her an encyclopedia of his thoughts. She wouldn't stop him now. "To...?"

"To take you to bed. Although I want that, more than you can ever imagine. So, I'm leaving now and asking you out again for tomorrow night."

"What time?" she asked, her voice nearly shrill.

"Six."

"Fine," she said and walked to the front door, not entirely sure why she was so darn ticked off.

"Okay, I'll see you then." He grabbed the files up in his arms, walked to the door, leaned over on his way out, giving her a peck on the cheek, and then exited.

She slammed the door behind him and then glanced over to the half-eaten cake on the table and the scattering of crumbs on the floor.

Her face cracked into an unwelcome and uninvited smile.

She couldn't hold on to her anger any longer.

She had another date with Dan.

Five

Dan knocked on Erin's front door at exactly six o'clock, holding a box of the best darn fried chicken and mashed potatoes in the county, and the dog by his side.

The door opened seconds later, and Dan was hit by how lovely Erin looked tonight dressed in jeans and a ruffled white blouse, her hair clipped back as blond waves touched her shoulders. Looking into her pretty aqua eyes made it hard for him to breathe, and that scared him silly, but not enough to stop seeing her. He wanted her in his life for as long as she was staying in Texas.

"Hi," she said. And then her gaze immediately shifted down to Lucky. "Oh, Dan. You brought him." She bent to pet the dog, and was greeted by eager wet licks on the chin. Her giggles touched something deep inside. She was obviously glad to see the pup.

"I hope it's okay."

She roped her arms around Lucky's neck. "More than okay. I'm good with staying in. What did you bring?" She was nuzzling the dog's face, catching up, giving him love. Her affection, aimed at the dog, was a heady thing to see. He could never fall for a woman who didn't like animals.

But was that what he was doing with Erin? Falling for her? "Fried chicken from The Royal Diner," he said. "I think you'll like it."

"Smells yummy. Come in. Did you bring files too?"

He had texted her that morning and she'd been in full agreement they should continue work on the case. He gave her a nod and walked into the cabin, Lucky staying back, waiting for Erin. "In my car. I'll get them later."

He hated having to combine his dates with Erin with work on the investigation, but it was necessary to catch the jerk and put his sister's mind at ease. No one knew when Maverick was going to strike again or who would be his next target.

"That's fine. We need to keep working," she said, closing the door and entering the great room.

She reached for the box in his hand. "I'll take that," she said, and their fingers brushed as she relieved him of the food. Her touch was like a match igniting, the sparks causing an electric reaction to his system. Damn. He was supposed to play it cool tonight. Dinner, work and then see where things would lead.

Dan had kicked himself a dozen times today for leaving Erin wanting last night. It had taken all of his willpower to stop their erotic cake buffet and shift her off his lap, halting a trip to the bedroom. And because of it, he'd been in a sour mood all day, anxious to get here and make up for lost time.

He followed Erin to the kitchen. Lucky was close on his heels and took to sniffing out the place. She set the food down on the counter and when she turned around he was right behind her. He'd shocked her, coming up so close, looking into her pretty blue-green eyes, breathing in her scent, which was a cross between fresh rain and roses and uniquely hers. "You're beautiful, Erin," he said, unable to hold back.

He took her face in his hands and stroked down her cheeks and as he leaned in close, her lips parted, inviting him in. "Dan," she whispered.

The plea in her voice put Dan at a loss. A man could only take so much, and when Erin looked at him like that, sweetly sultry and so damn arousing, he made a decision. He brought his mouth down on hers and kissed her and kept on kissing her, until she was laboring hard for breaths. He was in no better shape. He inched away, giving her room to breathe, brushing a stray blond tendril off her cheek. She peered up at him, her gaze connected to his without so much as a blink of the eye. "Are you hungry?" he asked.

"Not for food."

Air exited his chest. Oh man. She was a temptation. And he was grateful for that. "Where to, sweetness?"

She folded his hand in hers and led him out of the kitchen.

There wasn't much Erin could do to stop the hurricane force connecting her to Dan. She held his hand—her heart rate clocking a new record for speed—and made her way into her bedroom. Rays of the moon sliced through the curtains, giving off light amid the shadows, the illumination enough for her to see the color of Dan's eyes.

"Here we are," she announced, keeping her voice low.

"Nice," he said, squeezing her hand. His gaze never touched upon the room, his eyes were solely on her. And oh, how *nice* and thrilling it was.

"Sweetness," he rasped, bringing her into the fold of his arms. Lucky intervened, sliding between their legs and she let a little chuckle escape. Dan didn't think it too funny. "Go," he told the dog, pointing to the corner of the room.

Lucky trotted off with his tail between his legs.

Dan kissed her then, impatiently as if he'd been starving for her. She felt the same way, the lightness of the moment vanishing into a fiery explosion of hands reaching for each other, clothes being shed and moans reverberating in the room. Dan slipped behind her, kissed the back of her throat and used one hand to cup her breast and gently massage the peak until heat stoked like wildfire between her legs. She whimpered and made a move to turn around, but Dan held her firm, his body fierce and protective, as he slid his hand down past her navel to sink into the oblivion of her folds. She fell back against him, the sound of her soft cries and his kisses echoing in her ears.

"Hold on," he whispered, but it was too late for holding on. She was in his grasp and he was making her crazy. Her body gave way, releasing quickly and forcefully, her cries amplified as she shuddered and splintered. It was the best and quickest she'd ever experienced and when it was over, she slumped in Dan's arms, her knees going weak from pleasure.

"Sweetness," he muttered, awed. His body rigid, his erection pressing her, he turned her around and kissed her deeply on the mouth. Then he lowered her onto the bed and came up beside her. It was only a minute before he was sheathed and inside her, holding her cheeks tight in his hands from underneath, raising her up easily and thrusting into her inch by inch.

Her teeth clamped down, the sensations so ripe, so raw. When she opened her eyes to look at him his desire burned hot and steamy, his thrusts harder now, more powerful. But his gaze never left hers, as if he was gauging her, making sure she could handle his size, his weight, his power.

"Yes," she cooed, accepting all he had to offer. Had it been this good the first time they'd made love at Hunt Acres? The sex, yes, but the feelings behind it didn't even come close.

"Erin," Dan whispered, and she wasn't sure he knew he called her name, he appeared that lost, that fully immersed in her.

The bed shook as he moved faster, his thrusts going deeper. His face contorted. She felt the same pressure build again within her. How could it not? Dan was her elixir, the catalyst to her wildest fantasies. Their joining was hot and amazing. Just looking at Dan, having his big body joined with hers was all she needed, to climb, to seek, to let go.

"Sweetness." His body surged, pushing her toward release again.

She gripped his shoulders, her fingertips going deep into his skin. "Dan."

And then his body broke apart, just as hers did. The mating timed perfectly, they rocked back and forth, huffing out each other's names.

"Oh man," he breathed out noisily. "That was effing great, sweetness."

"Yeah." It was the understatement of the year.

"You okay, baby?"

She looked into the clearest, most amazing blue eyes and found something there she hadn't seen before. Something, she was afraid to name. "I'm more than okay."

Dan laughed and folded her into his arms.

Lucky took that second to jump onto the mattress and make himself comfortable at the foot of the bed.

This time, Dan didn't seem to mind.

* * *

A short while later after dinner, Erin sat cross-legged on the bed and Lucky scooted close to her, laying his head on her lap. She scratched him under the ears and the dog rewarded her by wagging his tail and licking her hand. "You sweet boy," she said, kissing the top of his head.

"Not sure if I should be jealous," Dan said, coming into the bedroom with a stack of files. They were both semidressed, Erin wore Dan's super soft flannel shirt and he'd put his jeans back on along with his white undershirt.

"Of him or me?"

"Both of you. You're gettin' pretty darn cozy together."

"Yeah, well, Lucky's special." She stroked the dog's coat.

"He must think you're pretty special too. You tossed him chicken under the table."

"Guilty as charged," Erin replied. Dan hadn't been wrong, Royal Diner's chicken was the best she'd ever had and she had no qualms about sharing with the dog. Those big brown eyes had gotten to her.

The mattress dipped as Dan set a knee on the bed and then climbed in next to her. "Is he gonna help us find the culprit in all these files?"

"He'll be our mascot."

"Yeah, well, I hated this creep Maverick before. But now that we've got to delve into these files tonight, when we could be—"

"Cuddling?"

Dan stopped to smile and wink. "Yeah, sweetness. That's what I was gonna say."

A rumble of laughter forced through her mouth. "You're a terrible liar."

"I know," he said, horse-collaring her closer and kissing the very top of her hair.

"It has to be done, Dan."

"True, but I don't usually end a date by breaking out folders."

"How do you end a date?"

He rubbed at the whiskers along his jawline and shook his head. "It's been so long, I can't recall."

Erin didn't really believe that. Dan was too handsome, too great a guy not to have females dropping at his feet. "You're lying again."

"I'm not. Chelsea says I'm picky when it comes to women."

"Oh." If that was a compliment, she was happy to take it.

"What about you?"

"What about me?" Erin asked right back at him. Her antennae were up. She didn't like talking about her love life. It was hard and awfully discouraging.

"You know what I'm asking." Dan's eyes went to a deeper shade of blue, the way they did when he got serious. He held her gaze firm and she couldn't look away.

"I do. It's…hard to talk about."

"You got your heart broken," he stated.

"I…did. You really don't want to know."

"Maybe I do."

She put her head down. "It's embarrassing."

"More embarrassing than getting dumped on your ass by a fake bull?"

"Yes," she said, a smile pulling her lips apart. "Okay. There was a bit of a scandal in Seattle and I was in the center of it."

This did not seem to shock Dan. She wasn't sure if that was a good thing or not, but he didn't blink or laugh or curse. He just stared at her, waiting.

His patience and willingness to listen encouraged her to speak. She went on to tell him about Rex Talbot and how they'd dated, how he'd led her to believe he was single and how, after a few months when his socialite wife came back into the picture and found out about their love affair, scandalized Erin's good name.

It was hard revealing this to Dan. She didn't really want him to know how stupid and gullible she'd been, but at the same time, it was freeing getting that off her chest. By revealing her secret to him, somehow she felt closer to him, giving him her bond of trust.

"So you never suspected he was married?"

"No. Maybe I didn't want to see the signs. Maybe I just wanted to believe him, no matter what I might have suspected."

"Why would you do that?"

She shrugged. "My folks have this amazing marriage. They respect each other and are honest about things. I grew up believing it was all possible."

"And now you don't?"

"I don't know what I think anymore."

Dan sighed and studied her face. Did he believe her? Was he thinking her a fool for not being more intuitive or questioning Rex's motives? In hindsight she saw some telling signs, but didn't pursue them at the time because she'd had faith in mankind. And then that faith had been shattered.

"I appreciate you telling me," he said quietly.

"I am not proud of it."

He blinked then and a question came into his eyes. He had something on his mind, but he wasn't going to ask. "I am over him completely."

He let air out of his lungs. "Okay."

The files he held landed with a thump on the nightstand and he turned to her. She looked at him carefully and felt his gentle force as he lowered her down onto the bed, tucking her into the curve of his body and holding her tight. Her eyes closed and she waited for him to move, to take her to places that made her forget the bad things. And when nothing happened, she whispered, "Dan, what are we doing?"

He kissed the base of her neck and whispered back, "Cuddling."

Tears immediately welled in her eyes and her throat constricted. She could only nod and press herself more solidly into the safety of his arms.

Dan took the shirt off her back, literally, since it was his shirt she'd worn as they'd made their way through a batch of TCC files tonight, after they'd made love and cuddled sufficiently.

"I've got an early appointment in the morning." He sighed and brought his mouth to her bare shoulders, planting tiny kisses there. "Or I'd love to stay and make you blush again."

"I don't blush," she said softly.

"You sure about that? 'Cause from this end, it's pretty damn thrillin' seeing your skin color up that way when we come together."

"Dan," she whispered, her body beginning to flush again, hearing his deep velvety smooth voice caress her with sexy talk.

He slid his arms through the sleeves of his shirt and let it hang off his shoulders. "God, I hate to leave you."

She grabbed his shirt with both hands and went on her tiptoes, giving him a brush of her lips. He dug in for more, deepening the kiss and when he was through her quiet sigh was more like a purr of absolute contentment. "I hate for you to leave too."

Naked but for a pair of silky panties, she was totally comfortable standing before Dan, allowing his eyes to roam over her and yes, see her flush of color again. See the want her body couldn't conceal. She was getting in too deep with Dan and on a self-defending note, backed away and put on her warm pink robe. "I'll walk you out," she managed.

He gave the keyboard a glance. "Do me a favor before I go?"

Anything. "Depends."

Dan's brow went up and she smiled coyly. She could be a tease when she wanted to be.

"Play for me. Just once, sweetness."

She wanted to say no. She was rusty and it was late and she wasn't ready. But the excuses in her head didn't play out. She couldn't deny Dan, not when he hadn't denied her anything tonight, except his heart. That, he seemed to keep under lock and key.

"Okay."

Dan picked up a ladder-back chair with one hand and scooted it over to the keyboard. With a flare of his arm, he gestured for her to sit down.

She took her seat and set her hands on the keys, getting familiar again. She hadn't played since she'd given her resignation at the school. It had been too difficult and she'd put that part of her life on hold for the time being. But now, she found that she really did want to share this with Dan. "What would you like to hear?"

"Your favorite. Whatever you enjoy playing."

She nodded and immediately knew what piece she would play for Dan. "This is called 'Kiss the Sky,'" she said quietly, getting her bearings on her seat, splaying her fingers out in front of her, giving them a good stretch. And as soon as her fingers touched the keys, she was off, flowing as the notes poured out and a sense of calm, not panic as she'd thought, seized her. She knew the song by heart. She'd written it.

Dan sat on the bed and out of the corner of her

eye, she saw him resting on his elbows, watching her. She thought having an audience would make her nervous. She thought all of her bad memories would come rushing back, but playing this song for Dan boosted her up, giving her a much-needed shot in the arm. She closed her eyes as the notes swayed her and yes, she was rusty to her critical ear, but the song still held its spirit and came through as a shining testament to her skills as a musician with each touch of the keys.

When silence once again filled the room, Dan was there, lifting her out of her seat and into his arms. She was bulky in her robe, but Dan brought her close and she looked into the solid blue sea of his eyes. "That was something," he said, his voice gravelly. "I didn't expect…to be dazzled."

She smiled. "I dazzled you?"

"From the second I saw you. But yeah, tonight, you dazzled me. You're very talented, Erin. And clearly, you love what you do."

"I guess. I forget how much I do love it."

"Well, now you know." He smiled with his eyes. "I've got to go. I'll call you tomorrow."

"Sounds good. I'll walk you to the door."

"Not necessary. You stay. Keep playing. You should always play."

And with that, and a kiss on the cheek, Dan was gone.

In the morning, Dan hummed the tune Erin had played for him as he drove to the Cattleman's Club.

His body was sated, filled with thoughts of the stunning woman he'd left some hours ago.

It was early, just after dawn, the rising sunlight blocked by big gray clouds forming overhead. The November air took on a bite, a foreshadowing of the winter days to come. He reached the club early enough not to be noticed and returned the files to their original cabinets straightaway. As far as finding any clues about Maverick, they'd come up with a big fat zero and it was disappointing.

But nothing about meeting Erin had disappointed. She continued to surprise him, each time they were together. She was a talented pianist and it was a shame she didn't play more. It was also a damn shame she'd had to resign her position at the school in Seattle too. It just confirmed his belief that life wasn't always fair. That sometimes, life could be cruel.

It had been cruel for his family when they'd lost their dad, even though it was many years after their mother had abandoned them. They'd taken some hard knocks along the way even after that, but he, Chelsea and Bradley had managed to survive. Still, they'd grown up motherless, robbed of a family life that could've been better, happier, on solid ground.

He'd learned a hard lesson then, ingrained in him since childhood. Don't get involved. Don't get suckered in. And you won't get hurt. It's the way he'd run his life up until this point.

Not that he wasn't glad he'd met Erin Sinclair. But she was going back to Seattle to live. He had known going in that their involvement was temporary. She had to know it too. She was gun-shy about commitment after what she'd gone through and probably had trust issues similar to his. Not that he blamed her about what happened in Seattle, but he wasn't sure she was over it entirely.

Dan exited the file room and drove into Royal for a breakfast meeting with some of the local managers of Hunt and Company. It was a routine meeting at the Royal Diner, but everyone from the waitresses to his most trusted employees had one thing on their mind, the upcoming storm.

"They say it could be a big one," the waitress said, serving plates of hotcakes.

"That so? I didn't hear." He hadn't. He'd been humming Erin's tunes on the drive into Royal this morning, not listening to weather reports.

"Yep, it's all over the news now. They're issuing warnings to the entire county. Could be as big as the storm that plowed through Royal a few years back," Jeb McNamara, his Dallas manager, said.

"They're warning about a tornado?" Dan asked.

"Yep, that's what the news reports are saying," Jeb added. "Could happen as early as this afternoon. They're closing the schools, just in case."

"Okay, then. We'll make this meeting quick, and then you folks all go on home. You don't need to be on the road when it hits. Keep your families safe."

The men and women around the table thanked him and they got on with the essential items on the agenda. Dan had a few key issues to discuss with the managers about Human Resources and the new rollout of his employee-of-the-month program. Dan was a believer in keeping the morale high at the company and worked with his family to see that his employees' needs were well cared for. After that discussion, he hastened his employees out of the diner, wishing them safe travel home.

Then he reached for his phone and speed dialed Chelsea's number.

"Hi, big brother," she answered. Caller ID had its merits. "I take it you heard about the storm?"

"Yep, just now. Where are you?"

"I'm at Bullseye Ranch with Brandee and Shane, so you don't have to worry. Shane's got everything under control. They have a shelter here, in case the storm gets out of control."

"Okay. I'm glad you're not alone. Stay safe." How well his sister knew him. He'd taken it upon himself to watch out for her over the years. Even though she was an independent woman, strong and fierce when necessary, she was still his baby sis. "How did your trip go?"

"It went well. I'll tell you about it when I see you. But it's all good. What about Bradley? Is the middle child still out of town?"

"Yeah, as far as I know. Last I heard from him, he wasn't coming home for a few weeks. Crescent Moon might be in the path of the storm." He needed to check out his family home. Crescent Moon was where they were all raised and it was Bradley's home now. "I've got to see to the animals, and let the staff go home."

"That's a good idea. Be careful, okay?"

"Always."

"Uh, Dan. Have you had much luck…with those files?" He pictured his little sis biting her nails like she did when she was kid and something bothered her. Like not having a mother to help her do her hair. Like not having a mom explain about touchy female things. Dan had tried, but hell, what did he know about pigtails and braids? He hadn't been the greatest at explaining the birds and the bees either.

"I wish I had better news for you, but Erin and I didn't find a thing that looked suspicious. We've been going over the files for two nights."

"You have, have you?"

"Yeah."

"I like Erin. It's awfully nice of her to do this for me."

"Yeah."

"Dan? What are you not telling me?"

"Nothin'."

"Nothin'? As in, 'None of your business, Chels'? That kind of nothin'?"

"Maybe."

"Maybe is good. I approve. Are you dating her?"

Air blew from his chest. Hell, he liked keeping things private but as sure as anything, his sis would probe him about Erin endlessly if he didn't shoot straight with her. And if he continued to see Erin, it'd be too hard to hide anyway in a small town like

Royal. "Alright, yeah. I'm seeing her, but it's a casual kind of thing."

"Casual? *With Erin*?" Chelsea laughed. As if she had some secret knowledge that *casual* and *Erin* didn't go in the same breath. "Dan, that's good. You've been alone too long."

"I'm not alone."

"Sure, sure, big brother. I know the drill. You have a company to run, a cattle ranch and your animals. You have it all."

She was poking fun at him. He should give her grief, but the storm was looming and he was glad enough that she was safe with her best friend Brandee. "Can't argue those facts. You called it, baby sis. Talk soon," he said, and after the phone call he jumped into his SUV, and instead of heading toward his family home, Crescent Moon, he sped toward the Flying E Ranch.

To Erin.

Six

As Erin took her morning jog along one of the Flying E's paths, she pounded out a pace that would clear her head. She'd woken up feeling restless, missing Dan. Running had always brought clarity and a new perspective, and today she needed that, more than anything. She'd just had a phone interview with the administrator at Lincoln Elementary. The call had gone exceedingly well, with no mention of the Rex Talbot thing. Apparently it had all blown over, and her old school had even given her an excellent reference. Her instincts told her she would love this job. It was everything she wanted; kids, music, a place to belong. She was a teacher and a musician, and when those two paths met, it was where dreams were made.

A Seattle Mariners sweatshirt and her adrenaline keeping her warm, she breathed in the cool crisp air. Clouds gathered above, gray and threatening. This wasn't new to her. Back in Seattle, cloudy days were the norm and never stopped her from jogging.

It was great having the wind at her back. She waved to ranch employees in the distance as she thundered past the guesthouses on the property, picking up speed, her legs aching in a good way. It was time to put her life back in order and not allow what happened with Rex tear her down anymore. Coming to Texas had been the best thing to happen to her. She needed this time to find her confidence, to find her pride and learn how to let go of the past.

As she rounded the corner leading to her cottage, she spotted Dan's SUV parked in front. Immediately a smile cracked at the corners of her mouth. A few more steps and yes, there he was standing on the porch.

He turned when he heard her footsteps and gave her an up and down perusal. The grim look on his face surprised her. Before she got close enough to meet his eyes, he said, "Where have you been?"

"Jogging," she replied. Wasn't it obvious?

"You don't take your phone when you jog?"

"I do, usually. Back in Seattle I always did. But since I wasn't going off the ranch I didn't think I'd need it. What's wrong, Dan?"

"I've been trying to call you for half an hour," he said, furrowing his brows in that adorable way, yet there was a serious something in his voice.

"I'm sorry you couldn't reach me." She wasn't sure why she was apologizing. "What's going on?"

"There's a storm coming, a big one."

She glanced at the sky. "I figured. Can we go inside?" As she unlocked the door and gave a little push, a sudden cold gust blew it open the rest of the way. She looked over her shoulder at Dan standing right behind her. "After you," he said.

She entered and led him into the parlor area of the great room. "I didn't think I'd see you this morning. Didn't you have a meeting?"

"I did," he said, "I sent my employees home."

"Wow, because of the storm?"

He nodded. "They needed to be home with their families."

She kept her eyes locked to his, wondering what was up. Was he here to warn her? "Dan, it's very sweet of you to come by. I'll be sure to stay inside until the storm is over."

He shook his head, and suddenly her hand was enveloped in his, his large palm wrapping around her smaller one. His eyes intense, his expression cast in worry, the look on his face completely drew her in. "Erin, this storm could be monstrous. It's happened once before in Royal, and there was devastation. I'd like you to come with me to Crescent Moon, my family home. I need to see to the animals and make sure the staff went home. There's an underground shelter there, in case it comes to that. I promise you'll be safer with me."

She blinked a few times, absorbing his words,

totally touched by his concern. "You came here to get me?"

He nodded, as if the idea was as natural as breathing. Did he think her a stray that needed rescuing? In some cases that was so true, he must look at her as a lost soul, a woman without direction at this point in her life. She hadn't told him about her job offer because it hadn't come through officially yet. And something else hadn't come through, as well. She had the pregnancy test to check out her symptoms, but hadn't the nerve to take it yet. Shelving that thought for the moment, she stared at Dan, rubbing at his jaw, waiting for her answer. He'd come here, guns blazing, ready to bring her to safety. What woman would refuse such a sweet and generous offer? The way she saw it, she had two options. She could sit alone in this cabin and wait out the storm, or spend her time with Dan at his family home and experience whatever adventure might await them.

When she thought in those terms, there really wasn't any option.

"Give me a few minutes to shower and change?"

"Just a few, Erin. And you might want to pack a bag, in case we have to spend the night."

"Okay and I'll call Will and let him know I'm going with you so he doesn't worry."

Fifteen minutes later, Erin was seated beside Dan in his black Escalade and as they headed off the Flying E, powerful bolts of rain began to pour down, slashing across the windshield. There was no preamble, no foreplay. One second the land was dry, the next the roads were slick and wet. Windshield wipers fought hard to clear Dan's vision as he drove with an expertise and caution she appreciated.

"Wow, you were right," she said, breaking the silence. "It's torrential."

"It will be, once the winds kick up. They estimate forty mile an hour winds. Did you bring your power umbrella?"

"I'm from Seattle, of course I did."

He laughed a little while concentrating hard on the road.

"How much longer?" she asked, after another long silence.

"Just another five miles and we'll be there."

The roads were relatively empty. Everyone from around here seemed to know how to brace for the storm. She huddled up tighter in her flannel jacket lined in lambswool.

"Oh damn," Dan said, staring out the windshield to his right. They passed a car on the side of the road, a woman in the driver's side with a phone to her ear. Dan immediately slowed the car and pulled over to the embankment. "Looks like she's stuck."

Erin strained to look into the car. "Dan, there's a car seat in the back. There might be a child in there too."

"Yeah, I see that. Stay put. I'll go check it out." Dan shoved the door open and climbed out, ducking his head and hanging on to his hat as he ran to the woman in distress.

Erin waited, strumming her fingers over the seat

cushion and after sixty seconds of not knowing, jumped down from the car and made a dash for it. When she reached the car, Dan gave her a look and then resumed working on the windshield wipers.

She waved to the woman who indeed had a toddler in a car seat behind her. Erin reached her driver's side window, rain pelting her. "Are you okay?"

"Yes, just a little frazzled," she said. "You're getting soaked. You want to get in?"

Erin didn't hesitate to get into the passenger side and introduce herself. "I'm Erin Sinclair."

"Judy Roberts. My wipers are on the blink. They're old, I should've had them replaced. I couldn't see a darn thing and I didn't want to take a chance with my son in the car."

"That's a smart move. How old is he?"

The little blond-haired boy seemed oblivious to his surroundings. He held his juice bottle and was busy staring out the window at the downpour. "Donny's two and a half. We were at the doctor's office. He's been sick and I thought I could outrun the rain."

Dan knocked on the woman's window and she lowered it. "Looks like I might've got them working again," Dan shouted over the rain. "Wanna give it a try?"

"Okay," she said. She turned on the ignition and the wipers cleared the windshield as they were intended. Relieved, the woman nodded to Dan. "Looks like they're working now."

"For now, anyway. If you want to try driving home, we'll follow you."

When the woman hesitated, Erin nodded. "We'll see you and Donny safely home."

"That's very kind of you. It's not far, just a couple of miles from here. Thank you both so very much."

"Glad to help," Dan told her. Then he gave her a nod. "Erin, let's go."

"We'll be right behind you," she assured Judy and then opened the car door. Her boots sunk into muddy gravel and angry drops of rain bombarded her face as she made a quick dash to Dan's car.

"Whew," she said, plunking in her seat and slashing her hand over her brow, drying her face the best she could.

Dan tossed his hat into the backseat. He was drenched and staring at her. Her hair plastered to the top of her head, her teeth chattering and her boots mud-soaked, she wasn't exactly female eye candy at the moment. But Dan's eyes were warm on her anyway. "It was nice of you to get out and help."

She pushed wet tendrils off her cheeks, finger-combing her hair. Hopefully it was an improvement. "I figured the woman might need a bit of moral support. Kinda scary getting stuck on the road in the middle of a storm, and with a child no less. But you're the one who stopped to help her, despite your need to get home."

He shrugged it off. "I couldn't just drive by. By the time someone got to her, the storm could've been deadly. Anyway, let's see if my fix-it job worked."

Judy pulled her car slowly onto the road and Dan followed behind her.

Thunder boomed overhead, the storm's rage a threat of what was to come.

"Is this where you grew up?" Erin asked Dan, getting small glimpses of Crescent Moon Ranch between intermittent swipes of the windshield wipers.

"It is," he said.

Even though big thick drops of rain obscured some of her vision, his family home still looked magnificent. A long winding ranch house stood out on a vast green meadow. As they drove in, a path of arching trees with intersecting branches meeting like linked fingers overhead led them to the home's entrance. "It's beautiful."

He nodded. "Home to me when I'm staying in Royal, although I spend most of my time at Hunt Acres."

Where he could be alone with his animals.

But wow, this place was a far cry from the humble little studio apartment Erin called home in Seattle, but home was home. And for the most part Erin liked her place. It was just the memories of Seattle that she didn't like so much.

Dan pulled into one of the five garages on the premises and parked the car. "I've got to check on the animals straightaway," he said. "After I get you inside and warm."

He was such a protector. He'd already done a good deed today in helping Judy and her son get home safely. And if she were being honest, Dan coming to get her at the Flying E could be added to his list of good deeds. She was safe with him, making the thrill of being with him that much more intense.

"Don't worry about me. I'll go inside and change into dry clothes."

"That'll work," he said. Dan grabbed both their bags and they got out of the car. He led her past the mudroom and a marvelous kitchen, to a room, she might guess by the floral feel to the space, that was once Chelsea's bedroom. "You can change in here. There's a shower too, if you want to warm up."

"Thanks, maybe I will. Where will you be?"

"I've got to make sure the horses are secure in the stable. Should be back in half an hour or so."

"Do I come looking for you, if you don't?" She smiled, but it wasn't a joke. She had a protective streak in her too.

"Not on your life. You stay put inside. This time, Erin, I need you to heed my warning. Don't go outside. As soon as I get back, I'll show you where the bunker is."

The tone of his voice brought chills. "You really think it'll come to that?"

"It might. Like I said before, the tornado that whipped through Royal a few years back did a lot of destruction."

He waited patiently, watching her closely. "You don't come outside, got that?"

Thunder boomed again, the weighty clouds crashing together in the near distance. Another chill ran through her and she couldn't let him go without lifting on tiptoes and giving him a wet kiss on the cheek. "Got it, but please don't take any chances out there."

"Never."

Telling Dan not to risk himself for the sake of his horses was like telling a papa bear not to protect his cub. She got that, and it scared her a bit but thank goodness he was a big strong beast of a man. "Hurry back," she whispered.

She followed him to the back door and after he exited, strode to the kitchen window, catching a glimpse of him heading to a structure some distance away, his head down, his steps rapid, trying to outrun the weather. When he was completely out of sight, she returned to the bedroom.

Chilled to the bone, she stepped out of her clothes quickly, grabbed her bag and entered the bathroom. Setting the shower to medium hot, she got in quickly and the spray hit her in warm bursts. Immediately, her frigid insides began to thaw. In a perfect world, Dan would strip naked and join her there, but that wasn't going to happen today. He was out in the cold bitter storm and she only prayed that he would return shortly. She'd make hot cocoa or coffee or whatever he wanted to warm himself up.

In such a short time, Dan Hunt had become an important part of her life. In all her crazy dreams, she would never have believed this would happen to her again. Especially while in Texas, of all places. She'd come with the firm resolve to give up on men, at least in the short term. But it was happening and she couldn't do much to stop it.

After her shower, she dressed in a warm black knit sweater and jeans and covered her feet with fuzzy socks. She strolled around the room, restless, trying to ease her nerves by concentrating on an oil painting on the wall of majestic horses racing through a canyon, their manes lifting, their hooves pounding earth. It was beautiful in its simplicity.

Her phone buzzed and she was grateful for the distraction. Dan had only been gone a few minutes, but it seemed like hours. She took a seat on the bed and picked up on the second ring, smiling. "Hi, Mom."

"Hi, honey." Her mother's calm voice was just what she needed at the moment. "How are you?"

"I'm doing fine," she answered.

"Dad and I just got your message. We were out on the golf course this morning. You know your dad, if he doesn't get thirty-six holes in every week, he gets grouchy."

A chuckle rumbled from her throat. Her father had to keep ultra busy, even in his retirement. "I figured as much."

"So, you have good news, I hear?"

"Well, like I said in the message, I think so. Will recommended me for a music director job at an elementary school in Seattle."

"That Will, he's such a wonderful man."

"Yes, he's been great. Anyway, they liked my résumé and I had a phone interview with them a little while ago. Just thought I'd give you a heads-up. I know you were worried about me. *I* was worried about me, but now it looks like things might straighten out."

"So if you get the position, you'll be moving back to Seattle soon?"

"Well, yes. But the job doesn't start until the first of the year."

"That's wonderful. Dad and I were planning on taking a few weeks to visit you. You just tell us when it's convenient and we'll be there. We can do one of those duck tours. I hear they're fun."

"Yeah, they are. And I'd love seeing you and Dad."

"Wonderful. So, are you still enjoying Texas?"

Thunder clapped overhead, an insanely loud smack that shook the house. Her thoughts immediately flashed to Dan out there somewhere, in this awful weather.

"My goodness, what was that?"

"Thunder. It's raining pretty hard here, but don't worry, I'm inside."

"Well, I hope so, Erin." It was her mom's way of giving a warning, using her name in that particular tone.

After a few minutes of catching up, Erin ended the call and glanced at her watch. Dan, whom she didn't mention to her mother, still wasn't back and it had been nearly thirty minutes. Erin's heart began to race. Every second that ticked by gnawed at her gut. Where was he?

* * *

Inside the stable, Dan grabbed his left arm and applied pressure to the thick slash as blood seeped through his fingers. He looked at the wound and decided he'd live. He'd sustained much worse in his time on the ranch. That last bout of thunder scared Suzette silly and the mare reared back, slamming him into the pronged side of the gate latch. The latch cut through the thick cloth of his coat and ripped his skin.

His arm burning like a son of a bitch, he gave the area one last glance around. He'd done all he could to secure the horses in their paddocks, making sure they had enough feed and water to sustain them through the storm, and then exited the stable. Instantly, rain pelted him in large hard drops. He kept pressure on his arm and made a run for it, heading for the house. The distant sound of sirens reached his ears and he stopped midstride to make sure it wasn't just the bellowing of the wind causing the ruckus. Nope, he hadn't been wrong. It was a tornado siren.

Dan continued on, making his way into the house. He found Erin there, at the back door with her jacket and boots on, looking guilty. He'd caught her red-handed, ready to come looking for him. He was too damn glad to see her to get mad at her. There was no time for anger, just action.

"Get your bag, Erin. We have to get into the bunker. The tornado siren is going off."

"I hear it but, Dan, your arm? You're hurt."

"It's nothing. Do as I say. We need to get going."

Within a few seconds, they were heading outside to the back end of the house and going down a flight of steps into the darkness illuminated only by his flashlight.

"Hang on a minute," Dan said, ignoring the pain in his arm. He scurried around and found two battery-powered lanterns. A flip of the switch and they were lighting the space about the size of his parlor.

"Dan," Erin said, her voice a little wobbly. "This place is fully equipped, right?"

"Yep, you'll be safe here. We've got everything from food to first aid kits."

"Well, then, sit down," she said, pointing to one of three cots along the wall. "And show me where the first aid kit is?"

"Over there, in that tall cabinet against the wall." He plunked down on a cot.

It was frigid down here, something Dan could soon remedy with a battery-operated room heater and thermal blankets.

Erin found what she needed and came to sit beside him, setting the supplies down on the cot. Nimbly and with care, she helped him remove his jacket and gasped aloud as soon as she caught sight of the wound from beneath his ripped shirtsleeve.

"Sweetness, it's not that bad."

Her eyes lifted to his, sympathy and worry marring her pretty face. Clearly, she didn't believe him. "I'm so sorry you got hurt."

"It's just a cut."

"It's more than a cut." She sorted through her ammo of bandages, antiseptic and creams and suddenly her breath caught. "I think this is going to sting."

She soaked the cotton balls in antiseptic. "I have to clean this up. I hope you're up on your tetanus shots."

"I am, and have at it. I'm a big boy."

She didn't look amused. Her face contorted as she dabbed at his wound. "You okay?" She looked deep into his eyes.

"Fine."

"You know it doesn't reflect on your manliness if you admit it hurts."

"It hurts." He smiled through the gut-wrenching stinging. Erin always delved deeper. She always wanted to bring out more of him. He didn't like to show the vulnerable side of himself. But lately…

"Sorry about this," she said, continuing to cleanse the wound.

"There's a butterfly bandage in there. When you're finished, put that on and that should do it."

She nodded. "I could've never gone into nursing."

Dan disagreed. "You would've made a good one. You're compassionate."

"I'm a wimp when it comes to someone I care about."

Dan let that sink in. He was already in too deep with Erin, but that wasn't stopping him any. No, she was like a pleasant addiction and if he was being honest, it wasn't just about sex anymore. He was constantly reminding himself that this thing with Erin had to be temporary.

"You're doin' just fine," he told her.

Gently, Erin put the butterfly bandage in place and then began wrapping his arm with a long piece of gauze.

"There," she said, staring at her handiwork. But every so often, her eyes would dip down to his bare chest and he tried like hell not to smile.

"Feels better already. Thank you."

"You're welcome."

"I'm goin' to be fine, Erin." He got up from the cot and walked over to one of the three cabinets lining the wall. In one, he found a white T-shirt and walked it back to the cot. "Help me put this on?" he asked.

"Of course."

He put the shirt over his head and she helped ease the sleeve over his sore arm. "You know I'm injured when I'm asking you to help me put my clothes back on."

She laughed. "I think I do. Why don't you lie down and get comfortable?"

"Don't mind if I do." He grabbed a thermal blanket out of a cabinet and sank down onto the cot. "Join me and I'll keep you warm."

"I have no doubt," she said.

He took up most of the narrow cot, but he opened his good arm and she curled up next to him. He breathed in the scent of her hair, rain fresh with a hint of something flowery and while a violent storm raged outside, all seemed peaceful in their little nook of the world.

Erin woke to her stomach growling. Embarrassed, she grasped her belly, hoping to quiet down the noise. Dan had dozed beside her, his face tranquil now, as she watched him sleep. It felt eerie in the dimly lit shelter. She wouldn't want to be in there alone, that was for sure. Having Dan next to her kept her calm. Outside the winds still howled, but the storm pounding the earth earlier seemed to have let up.

Her tummy rumbled again. Dang it. She didn't want to disturb Dan's rest. Untangling herself from Dan's good arm, and easing off her part of the blanket, she sat up on the cot. Cool air struck her skin and goose bumps rose up on her arms. But it wasn't enough of a deterrent to make her curl back under the blanket and risk waking Dan with her very loud hunger pangs.

She planted her feet on solid ground and then tiptoed toward the cabinets and quietly opened each door until she found the mother lode of survival foods. Scanning over the well-equipped stash, she noted most Mylar food packages required boiling water. Delving farther inside, she came up with a box filled with packets of banana chips. Ugh, not a fan. All she wanted was a snack, something to quiet her noisy stomach pains. And then she remembered she'd brought her purse down there.

She scrambled to the floor and sifted through all the items in her bag, finally coming up with two foil packages of vanilla-flavored teething biscuits. She had kept a supply for Faye tucked in the bowels of her purse, never knowing when the baby would need them. Often, Erin would eat them along with her. They were actually pretty tasty.

She sat on the floor, unpeeled the foil wrapper and dug in, remembering her times with Faye. It was just a month ago that she'd been her nanny, happy to have a job and a little one to watch over. It could very well be that Erin would have a little one of her own to care for. She wouldn't know until she got up the nerve to take the pregnancy test she'd brought home the other day. She just wanted to give it a little more time. She didn't want her relationship with Dan to be defined by what she found out in that test.

She had time. There was no sense in panicking or getting ahead of herself.

"You hogging that cookie all for yourself?" Dan's voice shattered the silence.

"Dan!" She hadn't heard him get up. He scooted next to her on the floor. "You're awake. How's your arm?"

"Better."

She gazed into his deep blue eyes and couldn't tell if he was telling the truth. "Really?"

"Yep."

Okay, she'd have to take him at his word.

"You didn't answer my question," he said, a teasing glint in his eyes. "You're holding out on me. Got any more of those cookies?"

She lifted the cookie to his face. "Yes. One more package."

"You sharing?"

"These are baby teething cookies, Dan."

"*You're* eating them," he said. "They must be good."

"They are, and of course I'll share them with you. On one condition."

Dan's brows rose in question.

"You tell me three things about your childhood that I don't already know."

He pulled back. "That's three conditions."

"True, but that's the deal." She waved the cookie by his nose again and he eyed it as if it was the most delicious melted chocolate-chip cookie in the world.

"I don't like to talk. Never did. Ever since I was a kid, I found myself relating more to animals than humans."

"That's one, although I really did figure that out about you already. Two more to go."

"My favorite color is aqua, a combination of blue and green that's rare and brilliant," he said, staring straight into her eyes.

"Um, that doesn't count," she whispered, melting a little bit inside. Dan was paying her a compliment. "Favorites aren't part of the deal."

He smiled and the warmth of his palm touched her face. "You making up the rules as you go, sweetness?"

"Maybe I am."

"Then maybe after all this, you're gonna owe me."

"What? A cookie?"

A gleam entered his eyes and suddenly they weren't talking about food anymore. "That too." As thrilling as that prospect was, she really did want him to share more with her about his life.

"Tell me," she whispered.

He put his head down, shaking it, and then lifted his lids to hers, his incredible blue eyes meeting hers, and in that exact moment, she knew he was ready to speak about his past. He cleared his throat and began, "My mother left us a week before Christmas. I was ten. It was hardest on me, because I was the oldest and really understood what that meant to our family. I spent a lot of time in the stables with the horses. But then I would come into the house and see my dad sitting in his chair, staring into space, and I knew we hadn't just lost our mom, but our father too. He was never the same after my mother left. He didn't rally. He didn't hug us and tell us it was all going to be okay. He was shell-shocked and broken. I helped raise Chelsea and Bradley. Dad sort of let me do it, giving me reign over them, because he couldn't cope with three children. He couldn't deal with the ranch, the family and the heartache."

"Do you know why your mother left?" she asked softly. She couldn't imagine it. And she didn't know if Dan would give her an answer, but every revelation helped her understand him better. His retreat into himself, the solace he found in animals.

"I didn't know why for a long time. But years later, before my father passed, he admitted that our mother had never really loved him. She'd never wanted a family. She was too free a spirit to be tied down. Dad said despite knowing that about her, he thought he could make her happy. They married young and he thought he had all the time in the world. That didn't ever happen. The old memories I had of my mom are tarnished by what I've learned about her from my father. She's off somewhere, traveling the world on her own terms. She never remarried, but has a cluster of friends she moves with."

Erin saw through the shield he put up to hide his pain. It was real. It was potent and very sad. "Have you spoken to her since she left?"

"No."

Erin took his hand and squeezed, connecting them, trying to absorb some of his pain. She was extremely close to her parents. They had a great relationship and even though Erin didn't see them on a regular basis, they were always there for her, whenever she needed them. There was something to be said about knowing deep down in your heart that your folks had your back, always. And Dan never had that. Her heart broke for that little boy, carrying the weight of his family on his shoulders.

"Dan, come with me. I have something better to give you than a cookie."

She rose, tugged him up and led him over to the

cot. Rain drizzled now, and from what she could hear outside, the major part of the storm had passed. But there was something else this shelter could give them, besides safety. And she was bound and determined to show Dan exactly what that was.

Seven

Two days later, Erin glanced out her bedroom window to a deep blue sky. The dark clouds that had hovered overhead for days were gone, and now beautiful white cloud puffs let the sunshine through. Everything outside had dried, the grass christened by rain grew greener, the leaves on the oak trees wavered in the breeze and the dark pounded earth was that rich deep red-brown again.

The storm that raged had left flooded streets especially in the flatlands and that included most of Royal, but there were no deaths and no major structural damage to the buildings and schools and roadways. Yes, there were more potholes on the streets, and some windows got blown out and a small sec-tion of town lost power for a short time, but for the most part, Royal weathered the storm pretty well.

We got lucky this time, Dan had said, after the storm had passed.

It touched her deeply that Dan had sought her out and made sure she was safe during the storm. He had a protective streak a mile long. She saw it in the way he'd wanted to find Maverick and make the guy pay for his crimes, and she saw it in the way he gathered up stray animals, bringing them into the safety of his home. What she didn't know was, how he felt about her. Did he lump her into his "stray" category, consider her someone who needed protection from fake bulls and torrential storms? Or did he care for her more deeply?

He hadn't shared any of his feelings with her. And it was beginning to really bug her. So much so, she was through trying to hide behind her fears. She had to confront her situation head-on. There were too many unknowns in her life.

Did she have a job? She'd had a phone interview with an administrator of Lincoln Elementary, but hadn't heard a word yet about the outcome.

Was she leaving Texas after the holidays? One way or another, she pretty much had to, didn't she?

And most important of all, was she going to have a baby? Dan's baby.

She hadn't gotten up the nerve to take a pregnancy test yet.

She trembled at the thought of being pregnant. What would Dan's reaction be? He made no bones about how he spent his life as a loner, a man who didn't make relationship commitments. A man who while in the quiet shell of the bunker yesterday, spoke sobering words of honesty, revealing the terrible pain of his childhood. She couldn't imagine growing up without a mom and dad supporting her, guiding her, loving her. No child should go through that instability and heartache.

"Oh, Dan," she whispered against the windowpane.

Her phone buzzed and she walked to her nightstand to pick it up. It wasn't Dan as she'd hoped, but it was someone she'd wanted to speak with, someone she was expecting. "Hello, Mrs. Lawrence. Yes, this is Erin Sinclair."

"Well, I hope I have good news for you. You are our first choice to be Lincoln Elementary School's new musical director. We'd love to have you on board."

Erin slid her eyes closed. This was what she wanted, it really was, but accepting this position meant leaving Texas. It meant leaving Dan. She had always planned on leaving, but now it was official and she needed a job. This job would allow her to do the two things she loved doing most, playing music and teaching children. It was a win-win.

"Thank you. I'm very happy to accept the position."

"Well, then, welcome to the staff of Lincoln Elementary."

"Thank you, Mrs. Lawrence."

"It's Shelly. We're not formal here at Lincoln."

"That's, well, it's perfect."

"We'll see you after the first of the year for a day of orientation. I'll be sure to send you all the necessary papers in the meantime. Just send them back in the mail when you're through."

"Will do."

After she hung up the phone, Erin floated around the cottage in a daze. This was great news. One month ago, she wouldn't have believed she'd ever get a chance to go back to teaching in Seattle and now the perfect job had landed in her lap. She was so thankful to Will for getting her foot in the door.

Erin still had a little more than a month here in Texas. A little more time with Dan. She wasn't ready to give him up. And just as that thought struck, a brisk knock resounded on her door and she jumped. Her surprise was instantly replaced by excitement. She knew who was on the other end of that knock.

She opened the door and there he was, her beast of a man looking stunningly handsome in a black snap-down shirt and weathered blue jeans. Everything about him lit her up and she matched his wide smile when their eyes locked. "Dan."

He strode inside, sweeping her into his arms. "Sweetness," he said, and nothing more. But Erin knew it was Dan's way of saying he'd missed her. He'd been busy after the storm and they hadn't seen each other since.

He took her face in his hands and touched his mouth to hers, claiming her in a soul-melting kiss.

A tiny whimper rose from her throat and all seemed incredibly right in her world. How could that be, when there were so many questions? More questions than answers, but when she was with him everything seemed to fall by the wayside and all she could think about, all she could feel, was how wonderful it was to be kissed by him. His raw powerful scent, his unbelievably firm lips and the taste of him were unequalled by anything she'd ever experienced.

The kiss lasted a good long while, and she relished being in his arms, having him tilt her face from side to side to devour her lips impartially and when it was time to come up for air, he used his teeth to take tiny nips of her mouth.

"Hi," she said with a hiccup of a giggle.

Dan smiled, staring into her eyes. "Sorry to barge in."

Was he kidding? "You're welcome to barge in anytime."

"Yeah?"

"Yeah," she said softly. "How's your arm?"

He rubbed the area that had been gashed. "Healing."

"I'm glad. It looked pretty bad in the shelter."

"It's not," he said. "It's been looked at."

Good. He didn't need her nagging him about it. Dan was smart enough to know his own body and to take care of it.

"Listen, I had an idea," he said. "It's a killer of a

day, lots of sunshine left and I wanted to take you riding with me."

"*Horseback* riding?"

He grinned at the note of fear in her voice. "Ever been?"

She shook her head.

"Wanna learn?"

"Sure. Of course. Now?"

"Yeah, we've come up empty on our search for this Maverick guy. From what Chelsea tells me Sheriff Battle and his team aren't having much luck either. We're at a dead end at the moment. Chelsea suggested that we try to clear our heads. Maybe gain a different perspective. Riding always does it for me."

"Really? Will Chelsea be coming?"

"Nope. She's busy. It'll be just you and me. If you're willing."

"Sure, I'll do anything to help clear your noggin." She tapped her fist onto his forehead several times.

He grabbed her wrist, a light beaming in his eyes. "Careful, or I might not catch you if the horse decides to dump you on your pretty ass."

Her eyes popped wide-open. "Dan?"

"Kidding, Erin. I've got the gentlest mare for you and you'll never be far from my side. Nothing's gonna happen to you. That's a promise."

She gave him a wary look, just to mess with his head. But she did believe that he would keep her safe. "Let me change clothes. Give me ten minutes.

And just for the record, nothing much clears my head when I'm with you."

Dan let out a rolling belly laugh and winked. "See you in ten."

Dan's menagerie came rushing toward them as soon as they climbed down from the SUV, Lucky leading the pack and heading straight for her. Once he got close enough, he flew through the air, nearly knocking her down. She laughed as her knees hit Hunt Acres earth and her arms wrapped around his neck. "Hey, boy. I missed you too."

He did a number with his tongue, soaking her face with doggy kisses. Normally, that was not something Erin enjoyed, a slobbering dog, but Lucky was special and they had a mutual admiration society going for each other. So she let the dog lap at her cheeks and chin before Dan pulled the dog off her. "Hey, buddy. I don't need the competition."

Erin giggled and stood up, surrounded by the other hounds. All were vying for attention. Dan picked up the terrier and gave her a hug, while Erin shared her attention between the other dogs as Romeo and Juliet looked on from their perches atop the porch railings.

Clearly the cats couldn't be bothered.

Dan came down on one knee beside her to pet all of his crew. They were equal opportunity lickers, and Dan came away just as doggy loved.

"They've missed you," she said.

"It's your fault. Keeping me away from home so much."

"Ah, so I'm the culprit."

"Yes, Miss Sinclair, you are." He gave her a dazzling look that warmed her up inside. Then Dan took her hand and led her into the house. He tossed her a towel and they washed their hands and face. He was a businessman, smart and efficient, but it was hard to remember that when Dan looked every bit the cowboy in jeans and Western shirts, a black Stetson pushed back from his forehead. He dazzled her with his raw appeal, and made her go soft and gushy inside with his obvious love of animals.

"Have a drink before we head out." He grabbed a pitcher from the fridge. "Ever had sun tea?"

"I don't think so." She wasn't so sure what it was. The only tea she drank came from a kettle and tea bags.

"It's rare in November, because we usually don't get warm days, but Ted and I love it so much, Darla puts it outside on sunny days and hopes for the best. The tea is brewed by the heat of the sun over a day or two. Makes the taste more clean and sweet." He poured her a glass. "Here, try it."

He brushed his hand over hers making the transfer, and Erin loved how Dan found every opportunity he could to touch her. She put the glass to her lips, the lighter scent wafting up to her nostrils and then she sipped, letting the flavor slide down her throat. "Hmm, I like it."

He nodded and downed half a glass in one gulp. "Satisfies."

It was such a Dan thing to say, she had to tease him.

"I'll say." She eyed him up and down, her lids at half-mast as she gave him a coy smile. Heat rushed up his face. She'd never made Dan blush before.

"Oh no you don't," he said, grabbing the tea from her hand and setting both glasses down. "You're not gonna tempt me outta that ride."

"I'm proposing a different kind of ride." She couldn't hold back the smile cracking at the corners of her mouth.

He pointed his finger in her direction. "Hold that thought," he said. "And come with me."

He took her hand and marched her toward the stables, where a young ranch hand was waiting outside with two horses. "Thanks, Toby."

"Sure thing, Mr. Hunt."

He took hold of both the reins. "I'll take it from here."

"Have a nice ride," Toby said.

"Thank you."

The young man tipped his hat. Texans had such nice manners.

"This is Trudy," Dan explained after Toby sauntered off. "She's a sweetheart. She won't give you a bit of trouble."

"I hope not." Suddenly, staring up at the mare Erin's bravado waned. "She's tall."

"She's average size. My horse, Titan, he's tall."

Erin couldn't argue. Titan was a giant of a horse. "Are you ready?"

She looked at her pretty mare marked with gray and white and nodded.

Dan rattled off a bunch of instructions but the main takeaway was for her not to panic, to show the horse who was boss and to keep her butt in the center of the saddle and her boots in the stirrups. She could do that. She really could.

With Dan's help, namely his hands on her butt, she was mounted and settled in the saddle, holding the reins.

Dan mounted Titan with the grace of a ballerina. Sitting at least two feet taller than her, he gave her a reassuring smile. "You ready?"

She inhaled a breath. "As I'll ever be."

This made him laugh. "You're gonna do fine." He gave Titan a command and he took off at a slow walk. Erin really didn't have to do a thing, Trudy began following behind.

"You okay?" Dan said after a quiet minute.

"Yep."

He turned around to look at her white-knuckling the reins, her face probably the same colorful hue. *Don't panic*, he'd said, so she made a big effort to calm her nerves and placed her trust in him.

"That's it," he said in his gentle animal voice. There were so many tones to Dan she was still learning. "We won't go far."

"How far is not far?"

"Two or three miles. There's someplace I'd like to show you."

Erin got the hang of it after fifteen minutes. Well, maybe getting the hang of it was not exactly right, but blood was beginning to flow back into her hands again, so that was progress. They left cattle and feed shacks behind and continued to go deeper onto Hunt Acres land where wildflowers and tall grass grew in abundance. The recent storms greened everything up Dan had said, and the combination of blue sky and colorful earth, fresh air and solitude did bring a measure of peace.

Dan pulled up when they reached a creek, flowing hard with rushing waters. Large rocks banked the creek on one side and the sound of the rush filled her ears.

Dan dismounted and came over to help her down. "Swing your leg over the saddle. I've got you," he said.

She slipped down from the saddle right into his arms. "Yes, you've got me," she whispered as she turned around to face him and stare into his eyes.

He stared back, blinking several times, and then kissed her quick and hard on the lips. "You did pretty darn good on Trudy."

"Thanks. I'm learning."

"Yes, you are."

He grinned, hooked his finger into her belt loop and tugged her along. "Let's go sit."

She followed him to a boulder, one of the few on

this side of the creek and took a seat beside him. "Are we still on Hunt Acres land?"

"We are." Dan's gaze roamed over the water, the trees dotting the area and the meadow beyond. "I used to come here as a boy. Would play in the water, or just come sit and stare out."

"By yourself?"

"Sometimes Bradley and Chels would come, but mostly I came by myself. Me and my horse."

"No dogs?"

He let out a chuckle. "Them too. Had this one mutt, half beagle, half something else, named Joey. He was my BFF. He passed on shortly after my mother left."

"You must've taken that hard. All those losses for a young boy." She took his hand and squeezed and stared down at their entwined hands.

"I...did, I guess." He shrugged, clearly uncomfortable with the subject.

"Is that why you don't let people get too close to you?"

His eyes snapped to hers, a denial on his lips, but then he nodded. "I suppose. Just doesn't seem worth it, you know? I mean, you had your heart ripped out too, back in Seattle. Do you think it's worth it?"

"I, um." What could she say? That *he* was worth it. He was worth the gamble, because she knew something that he didn't know. She could see into his heart. He was one of the good guys, but he wasn't willing to take another chance. He obviously didn't think *she* was worth it.

Chelsea was right. Riding out to the far reaches of Hunt Acres, with the blue sky overhead and the air fresh from recent rains, did clear her head. "Dan, I have something to tell you."

Her somber tone had Dan lifting his gaze to hers quickly, a note of fear in his eyes. She'd never really seen that look on his face before. Did he think she was going to declare her undying love? No, she knew better. But she did care for Dan. Very much. She could no longer deny her feelings. She'd fallen hard for her Texan.

"What is it, sweetness?" he asked quietly.

"I was offered a job as musical director for a school in Seattle."

Dan waited a beat, his expression unreadable.

"I start the first of the year."

He nodded. "Congratulations. You'll be doing what you love to do."

"Yeah, that's true. So, I'll be leaving after the Christmas break."

"With a job waiting for you," he added.

"Yes."

"It's what you wanted, Erin."

Dan made it seem so logical, so absolutely clear, when right now gazing into his incredible eyes, nothing seemed clear at all.

"Let me take you out to dinner tonight to celebrate."

Sure, why not? She wasn't going to delude herself into thinking this little fling she was having with

Dan, meant anything more to him than having a good time together. "That would be nice."

The wind kicked up, the afternoon sunlight beginning to wane and she shivered.

"Here, put this on," he said, removing his suede jacket. He helped to put it on over her bulky sweater. "It gets chilly this time of day out on the range."

She cuddled into his jacket, putting her nose to his collar, breathing in his scent and wanting to cry. But she didn't dare. She held her tears in check. "Thanks."

She couldn't fault Dan. He'd always been honest with her. She'd known from the beginning that he wasn't a staying kind of man. He'd practically told her so on the first night they'd met and Erin had too much pride to be one of those clingy women who wouldn't let go.

"Let's head back," he said. "Get you warmed up."

"Sounds good," she said. "I sure could use some warming up."

Dinner had been fantastic, champagne flowed and Dan couldn't have been more attentive, toasting her new position at Lincoln Elementary. But as he wound around the car to open her door, Erin wondered, what now?

Dan didn't seem to have any such qualms. He helped her out into the chilly night air, wrapped his arm around her waist, cradling her close, and walked her to the door. "Would you like to come in?" she said, not sure if she should be asking. It wasn't as if they had any future, but then, there was always right now.

"Would love to."

One look in his eyes and she was a goner. She nodded and inserted the key into the lock and entered the darkened room. Dan removed his coat and walked over to snap on a lamp in the parlor area. "It's a great night for a fire."

She hadn't used the fireplace since she'd been there. "Sounds perfect."

Dan moved to the wall-to-ceiling stone fireplace and set about lighting a fire, while Erin took their coats and hung them in the entryway closet. They looked so settled there, the two coats brushing up against one another, side by side. She shouldn't get used to seeing them that way…just a few more weeks and all this would seem like a dream, a perfect, sweet, sensual dream.

"I'll make coffee," she said and headed to the kitchen.

Minutes later, the fire was snapping, casting the room in a golden haze and the scent of coffee flavored the air. "Here you go," she said, handing Dan a steaming mug.

"Mmm." He took a seat on the rug in front of the hearth and gestured for her to sit next to him. Together they stared at the new flames erupting, sipping coffee quietly.

"There's a Thanksgiving dinner at the Cattleman's Club this week. Chels will probably be there along with some of the friends you've already made here in Royal. Would you like to join me?"

"You're too late, Daniel Hunt. I've already been asked to go."

Dan put his mug down, a look of confusion marring his chiseled face. "What? Who? Do I need to beat up the guy?"

She chuckled softly. She loved being in the position to surprise Dan and she had the feeling it wasn't all teasing on his end. Her ego could stand seeing him being a tiny bit jealous. "Maybe. Will Brady's already asked me to go."

"Will? He already has a girl."

"He does. One I like very much."

"But, you'll be my date, right?"

"If you insist," she said, smiling.

"I do." He took up his mug again and sipped as if to say the subject was closed. Erin did the same, keeping both hands wrapped around the mug to keep warm. But in reality, sitting next to Dan was enough to make her sizzle inside.

He turned his attention to her, brushing her hair aside and nuzzling the back of her neck, planting moist delicious kisses there, and her arms broke out in goose bumps.

"Erin," he murmured.

"Hmm?"

"You're beautiful in firelight."

She smiled, and a moment later he wiped it away with a breathtaking kiss. She was in deep and didn't want to get out. She was totally ready for whatever the night would bring.

On a labored groan, Dan pulled her into his lap and turned her so she straddled him. Heat from the fire scorched her face as his kisses continued to flame her body. They were all hands, reaching to pull off each other's clothes. Garments flew through the air and landed who knew where. Bodies brushed, the initial contact so mesmerizing, so intensely beautiful, that it felt new, as if it was their first time.

Dan began touching her naked skin, lapping at her breasts, stroking her thighs, making love to her whole body with his hands, with his mouth. She touched him too, running her hand up and down his firm, ripped torso. He was broad and tough, there was so much of him to touch and the flat of her palms explored every inch of him.

The fire blazed and crackled, the only other sound heard above their gritted moans. Erin gave Dan her all, openly loving him with a freedom she'd once kept hidden and reserved. Her love for him was different than what she'd felt for Rex. Now she knew what real love felt like. Even though it wasn't returned, it still hummed in her heart and gave her a tiny shred of hope. In the moment. While her rational side was put on hold.

Don't think, Erin. Just feel.

And that's what she did. She felt every tingle, every jolt, every earth-shattering second of his love-making. The threads of the rug tickled her back as he laid her down beside the hearth. He came over her, a tower of a man silhouetted in shadows, so handsome and powerful, and she watched as he sheathed himself. She kept her focus on him as he nudged her legs apart, caressing her core, making sure she was ready and she held her breath as he sank inside, joining their bodies.

"Ah, sweetness," Dan murmured reverently, as if it was the best feeling in the world.

"Dan," she whispered softly, reaching up to touch the gruff stubble on his face. Firelight reflected off his ocean-blue eyes, making them gleam and in the next moment, he was moving inside her, filling her up and touching the sensitive layers welcoming him deeper.

Dan's body encompassed her and she began touching him, grazing his shoulders, sinking her fingers into his back, roaming, seeking, owning. He was hers right now, fully and completely and she relished every second with him.

And when they climaxed, reaching a solemn, soul-pounding peak, cries poured out of their mouths in unison, beautifully sweet, sensual sounds that echoed against the walls.

"Erin," he said, brushing hair from her cheeks and dotting her face with quick loving kisses. "You are incredible."

"Ditto," she said and giggled at her use of that dated term.

"Ditto?" He laughed too and grabbed her around the waist and rolled her on top of him. They lay there skin to skin, body to body, smiling and staring into each other's eyes.

She knew she was more to Dan than his bed buddy. She could see it in his eyes, but Dan had been wounded, maybe beyond repair, and that made her sad suddenly.

"Hey, what's wrong?" he asked, picking up on her mood.

I'm going to miss you. "Nothing." She put on a smile. "Everything's good."

"You sure?"

She nodded and just like that, the fire that had blazed so hot died out, the embers lending zero heat, and she trembled.

"You're cold. Let's get you into bed."

Dan didn't wait for her to answer, he simply picked her up and carried her to the bedroom.

Dan woke before Erin, his eyes opening to a stream of new dawn light working its way through the shutters. She was cuddled up beside him, her citrus clean scent mingling with his body heat, creating a unique blend of sated sex and sweet woman. Her passion was addictive and something he never wanted to let go.

He'd never craved a woman like this. Hell, he had to admit that being with Erin meant more than physical satisfaction. She was fun, and good and smart and all those traits made something as simple as a ride on horseback into a monumental memory.

Watching her sleep, her breaths steady and slow

and peaceful gave him a sense of belonging that he'd not experienced before. He wanted this woman in his life. He could deal with that, because she was leaving in a month's time and though it would be hard, he would have let her go.

Wanting was one thing.

Needing was another.

He didn't do need. Not ever again.

He closed his eyes to squeeze away the pain he'd felt after his mother left. She couldn't cope with having kids and a family life. She needed something different and often Dan wondered if he was cut from the same cloth. Had he inherited her inability to commit or had her leaving molded him into that kind of man?

Erin stirred, turning away from him, and he unlatched his arms from her waist. "Sleep, baby," he whispered and rose quietly, tucking her in tight to keep her warm.

He padded softly to the bathroom and closed the door. Without hesitation and trying to make as little noise as possible, Dan ran the water in the shower and stepped inside to a brisk morning wake up. He deliberately ran a lukewarm shower in the mornings to keep his wits sharp and focused at the start of the day.

After he dried off, Dan wrapped the towel around his waist and went in search of a toothbrush Erin recently kept handy for him. He couldn't find the dang thing, and as he shuffled things out of the way, he noticed a long rectangular box sticking out behind several bottles of lotion.

Pregnancy test.

He blinked several times and ten questions raced into his head. His chest pounded and his breaths became short labored bursts. What was going on? Was Erin hiding something from him? They'd been cautious, hadn't they?

He couldn't let this go. This had a direct effect on both of them. As he exited the bathroom, he held the test in his hand, and then sat down on the bed beside her. The mattress dipped and she stirred again. She seemed to sense him sitting there and her eyes opened slowly. Adjusting to the light, she squinted a bit and as she focused on him, she gave him a sweet smile.

"Morning."

"Mornin', sweetness."

"You're up early."

He nodded. "I am. Took a shower."

"Without me?"

He let that comment go. "How are you feeling this morning?"

"I'm perfectly fine. What's up?"

"Uh, is there something else you want to tell me?"

She blinked and stared at his somber face. "What do you mean?" She scooted up in the bed, rested her back to the headboard and covered her bare skin with the sheet.

She was fully awake now, her eyes wide and questioning.

He held up the pregnancy test. "I found this in the cabinet while I was looking for a toothbrush."

Her cheeks flamed, color rising rapidly on her face. "Oh, Dan."

"What's going on? Do you think you're pregnant?"

"No. Yes. I don't know."

"You don't know?"

She ran her hands down her face, pulling at the skin, and began shaking her head. "The truth is, I'm late. And I bought that as a precaution, but I've been waiting for the right time to take the test. I, uh… Oh, Dan. I wasn't hiding anything from you. I'm just not sure. My life has been kind of crazy lately, you know?"

"I do know," he said, sympathizing with her. "I get that you've been in turmoil, but don't you want to find out, and erase one more unknown in your life?"

"You want me to take the test now?"

"We need to know, Erin, but I won't pressure you. Too much," he said, unbelievably calm considering his gut was churning at breakneck speed. He could become a father. He could have a child. Something he'd never considered for himself. Something that should scare him silly, but Erin was the one who needed comfort, not him, so he kept his cool and became the voice of reason. "Whatever the outcome, you're not in this alone."

"Thank you for that. I think you're right. We should find out."

"Together?"

"Yeah, together." She sighed and gave her head a nod, a sudden determined look beaming in her eyes. She offered up her palm and he laid the box in her hand. "Give me a few minutes."

Minutes, which seemed like hours later, the bathroom door opened and Erin walked out, holding the pregnancy stick. He stared at her, her face giving nothing away. "Take a look," she said. "I think you'll be relieved."

He gave it a glance. "It's a negative reading."

"I'm not pregnant."

There was no such relief in her voice. Instead she'd spoken softly, her tone resigned.

He had to tread lightly here, her emotions were important to him, and hurting her was never something he wanted to do. He wasn't about to jump for joy. It surprised him how the relief he felt mingled with a measure of disappointment. How, if he had been the right kind of man for her, he would've been happy to have a baby. Erin's baby. It would mean that she'd stay, that they'd build a life together for the sake of the child. But now, they could go on the way they'd been going, enjoying their time together until she had to leave.

He wasn't heartless. He'd miss her terribly, but now he knew what his future held, and that was something he needed to know at all times. "At least we know now."

She nodded. "Yes, at least we know."

There was a touch of sorrow in her voice, and Dan realized something. Erin loved children. He knew how much she'd loved being nanny to little Faye Brady. She was a natural, and she would've made an amazing mother to their child. But she'd be a mom one day, he was sure, and she'd be happy in the role of wife and mother.

That disappointment he experienced a moment ago came rushing back stronger now. How had he gotten in so deep so fast? "Come back to bed. Let me hold you."

"You want to cuddle?"

A damn chuckle escaped, not that any of this was funny. "Don't sound so surprised. We've cuddled before."

"True, and I think you're an expert at it. But I think I need some time alone right now."

"Are you sure, sweetness?"

"Yes, I'm sure. I'll take a rain check on that cuddling."

"Anytime."

Dan dressed quietly, gave Erin a long reassuring kiss and walked out the door, a hollow feeling eating at his gut as he started his car and drove away.

Eight

"Just break off little chunks of butter, and squeeze the flour and butter between your fingers. It's a trick I learned from the Baking Channel and it works every time," Chelsea said to Erin as they stood next to each other in Chelsea's kitchen. It was the day before Thanksgiving and Erin was here to help bake the pies for the Cattleman's Club dinner. "The pie crust always comes out really tender that way."

"For you, maybe," Erin said. "I've never baked a pie from scratch before. My expertise is sticking a frozen pie in the oven and hoping the crust doesn't burn."

Chelsea laughed. "You're doing great, Erin. And I'll show you a trick later and you'll never burn another crust."

"From your lips to God's ears."

"I'm glad you decided to come over this morning and help me make these pies. It's more fun doing this with a friend."

Erin blew a wayward strand of hair off her face. "Just how many are we making?"

"Six."

"Six? Oh my goodness. That's enough to feed the entire town."

"Yeah, something like that. I was elected to bake the pies for TCC's Thanksgiving dinner. And we're making cookies too. I hope you didn't have hot and heavy plans with my brother today."

"Nope. Not a one. Today is a good day to wrangle me into baking with you."

"Is that so? So what's my brother up to today?"

"He texted he had a pile of work to catch up on today. I probably won't be seeing him."

"Really? Hmm."

"What?"

"It's just that you two are sorta perfect together."

"Sorta perfect? What does that mean, Chelsea?"

"It's just that Dan's been happy lately. Happier than I've seen him in a long time. He doesn't tell me much, but I can hear it in his voice. And when he mentions your name, his voice goes gooey soft."

"Nothing on Dan is gooey soft," she blurted, then slapped her hand to her mouth. "I didn't mean…"

Chelsea threw her head back and laughed. "TMI, Erin."

"I know, I'm sorry. I keep forgetting he's your brother."

"But you do like him?"

"Yeah, I do. He's an amazing man. But—"

"I know. He can be attentive and aloof all at the same time."

"You got that right, sister." Erin put both hands into the bowl and squeezed and molded the pie dough. "So what kind of pies are we making?"

"Cherry, apple, pumpkin, of course. And pecan. It isn't Texas if we don't have pecan pie. It's Dan's favorite."

"I didn't know that."

"We grew up on pecan pie. Of course, ours were store-bought. We didn't have a mother around to do any baking for us. But Dad tried his best. And we managed okay."

"So now you're making up for it, right, Chels?"

"Yep, six pies for our TCC family. But you're gonna make Dan his favorite."

"No way. What if I screw it up?"

"You won't. I'll be instructing you all the way. And Dan will enjoy it all the more knowing you made it for him."

She didn't have the heart to refuse Chelsea. She'd been such a good friend to her and she loved being included in the Thanksgiving festivities.

"Trust me, you'll do fine," Chelsea added. "Look at that dough you just made. It's perfect. Now gather it all up and roll it out."

Erin wielded the rolling pin, getting better and

better at smoothing out the dough to an eighth of an inch thickness, all the while copying what Chelsea was doing beside her. They made a good team, cutting up apples, making cherry filling, opening a can of pumpkin and finally lightly roasting pecans. When they were through, hours had passed and both of them were dotted in flour and slightly exhausted.

"That's hard work," Erin said, slashing her arm across her brow.

"Yes, but look at the gorgeousness of our pies."

"I have to admit, they are pretty, all golden brown and sweet smelling."

"We done good."

"Yes, and it was fun," Erin admitted.

"It's past time for lunch. I'm starving," Chelsea said.

"I wish I was. I taste-tested all the pie fillings."

"You need to eat, my friend. Don't forget, we have cookies to bake this afternoon."

"Okay, nourish me," she said. "I should eat something that's not full of sugar."

"I've got chicken salad in the fridge."

"Sounds good to me. So what kind of cookies are we baking later?"

"Chocolate chip, oatmeal raisin and snickerdoodles."

"Is that all? Piece of cake," Erin said.

Chelsea grinned at her snarky comment. "Oh, and I almost forgot, chocolate fudge macadamia nut."

"I know, Dan's favorite, right?"

"Well, honestly that guy can pack it in. He loves them all."

"Well, at least he loves something," Erin muttered under her breath and slanted Chelsea a look, hoping she hadn't heard her comment.

"I hear you. Dan's a bit of a hard case. But I know he cares deeply for you."

Erin dropped the pretense. Chelsea was fast becoming one of her best friends and she couldn't stand not being open with her. "Sure, he cares for me, Chels, but that doesn't make my world go round."

"What would?" she asked, softness entering her eyes.

"I've fallen for him."

"Oh, I didn't realize it's gone that far."

"He pretty much told me from the beginning he's not into permanent relationships. So doesn't that make me a dope for not listening to him?"

"No, it makes you human." Chelsea took her hand and squeezed gently. "Dan's a great guy and I love my brother dearly, but he has hang-ups. Rightfully so, since after my mom left and Dad died, Dan took the reins and practically raised us. It was a lot for him, and he never faltered on his duties at Hunt and Company, either."

"He's got all he needs," Erin said, wistfully.

"I don't think so. He needs more in his life. Like I told you earlier, you two are perfect together."

Chelsea gave her a hug she sorely needed. Chelsea didn't know about the non-pregnancy, but Erin was still smarting about it. A part of her would've loved having Dan's child. The realization of how disappointed she was had dawned on her the second Dan walked out her door yesterday. She'd shed tears, her heart breaking at what could have been. An unwanted pregnancy wasn't ideal in any case, but that was the thing. She would've welcomed the news, had she been carrying his child. "Obviously we're not."

"*Obviously*, my brother needs a swift kick in the ass. As do others."

"You're talking about Maverick."

Chelsea nodded, a somber look on her face. "Yeah, him."

"A kick in the ass is way too easy for him," Erin said.

"I'd like to see him with a permanent place in prison."

"It's hard to get over, isn't it, Chels?" Erin asked. Though she'd been violated too, by a man who lied and betrayed her, Chelsea's ordeal seemed more painful. To have her privacy invaded like that for all the world to see?

"I can't even begin to tell you what goes through my mind sometimes. I feel like I've been personally assaulted. It's almost physical. Even though I put up a brave front, it still hurts. But you know, it's Thanksgiving and I don't want to let him ruin my holiday."

"You're absolutely right. Let's not give him another thought. Besides, you mentioned you were going to feed me."

"I most certainly am. I need to fuel you up for cookie making." Chelsea opened the fridge and pulled out a bowl of chicken salad, her mood lightening up a bit.

"I'm only slightly better at baking cookies, than making pies. Fair warning."

"I'm so not worried." Chelsea filled two plates with chicken salad and sourdough rolls and brought them over to the table. "You're good at everything you do."

"Thanks and I mean that."

"You're welcome. Now let's have a seat, take a load off and eat our lunch."

Erin was grateful for the distraction, the friendship and the meal.

Six pies and eight dozen cookies later, Erin plunked down on Chelsea's sofa, almost too exhausted to put pizza to mouth, but the scent of garlic and pepperoni tempted her growling stomach enough for her to lift a piece out of the box and take a bite. "Oh, yum," she said.

Chelsea sat on the other end of the sofa, facing the flat screen television flashing a scene from the iconic holiday movie, *Miracle on 34th Street*. "Oh, that's good," she said, chewing her own cheesy piece of pizza. "Nothing like pizza and a Christmas movie to relax you."

"I know, right?"

"Thanks again for all your help. It's a daunting job but—"

"Somebody's got to do it."

She chuckled along with Chelsea. "I can't imagine all those desserts going after eating a big turkey meal."

"Believe me, they'll go. The club gets a big crowd on Thanksgiving. I'm sorta wondering if we shouldn't have more."

"More what?"

She gestured with her palms up. "Everything."

"Bite your tongue, Chelsea."

"Yeah, you're right. I'll shut up now and watch the movie."

Two bites later, Chelsea's phone chimed. "I bet it's Brandee. We text wedding stuff all the time," she said. "Excuse me a sec."

Chelsea was going to be Brandee's maid of honor. She'd talked about the Christmas wedding on Brandee's Hope Springs Ranch as they'd baked this morning. According to Chelsea, Shane Delgado, the groom, was a dreamboat. It all sounded so romantic and sweet.

But as Chelsea looked at the screen, reading the text, she shook her head. "It's not Brandee, after all. It's Dan. My brother's on his way over. He says he needs to speak to me about the case."

"Really? Maybe he's on to something." Erin sat upright and grabbed her purse. "I should go."

"No way. You're a part of this too. You don't have to run off. Dan won't mind you being here."

But she did. After last night, she found she needed time to sort out her feelings. Whenever Dan was around, her thought process faltered. She stood up. "But it's getting late. I really should be going."

There was a brisk knock on her door. "That was fast," Chelsea said, glancing toward the front door. "And please don't rush off. Dan will be glad to see you."

It would look weird if she chose to leave the second Dan arrived. Not that he'd given his sister much notice. She figured siblings could do that to each other, not stand on ceremony and show up at a moment's notice. "Here, please pause the movie," she said, handing Erin the remote. Erin sank back down on the sofa, pushed the button and froze an image on the screen of a department store Santa talking to a little girl.

"Something smells good in here," Dan said, his voice carrying into the room.

"Cookies, pies and pizza. Take your pick," Chelsea said.

Erin stood up and turned to give him a smile. "Hello, Dan."

"Hey, Erin," he said in that deep baritone, and her heart did a little flip. He looked good, as always, but his eyes were rimmed with red, as if he really had worked his butt off today. "I didn't know you'd be here."

"Chelsea invited me this morning."

"You mean, she conned you into baking with her?"

"Erin helped me make every single pie and all the

cookies today," Chelsea said. "She made you pecan pie, bro. But you don't get to taste it until tomorrow."

"Mean woman."

Chelsea gave her brother a grin. He made a face, and then turned to Erin, his eyes softening. "You made me pecan pie?"

"I tried."

"She did a great job. The pies are beautiful and I know they'll taste great."

"I'm sure they will," he said.

"Hey, Dan, we have plenty of pizza. Have some, if you're hungry."

"I think I will. Didn't have much time to eat today."

He walked over to a chair, and waited for Erin and Chelsea to sit down before he sat down adjacent to them.

"So what's up, big brother?"

He glanced at Erin and then focused back to Chelsea. "I stumbled upon something today regarding the investigation I thought had merit. I was speaking to a business associate today, you know Thomas Worley, right?"

"Yes, I know him. He's an attorney and a member of TCC."

"Yep, and as we got to talking he mentioned a man from a few years ago who'd been tossed out of the club for unruly conduct. Apparently, this guy was foulmouthed and verbally abusive to some of the women workers. One waitress filed a harassment claim against him, but it turned out he was Brentley

Jamison, the son of a US congressman, so he was quietly ejected from the club and his records were wiped clean. Tom doesn't know what happened to the guy and he didn't represent either party so he was free to tell me about it. It could lead somewhere, so I gave all the information I had to Royal PD and ran it by Gabe Walsh."

Dan explained to Erin that Gabe, being ex-FBI and owner of his own personal security firm, The Walsh Group, was more than capable of getting to the bottom of this.

"Chels, I thought maybe you might know something about this guy? Have you ever met Brentley Jamison?"

"No," Chelsea said. "I've heard the name, of course. His father was in Congress a long time, but I never met either one of them before. Still, it's worth a try."

Dan began nodding. "This guy's under the radar and it's worth checking into. They should know something in a day or two. He can't be hard to track down."

"Thanks, Dan," Chelsea said. "I know you both have tried hard to find the jerk."

Erin nodded. "I hope it's sooner rather than later."

"Yeah, me too," she said.

Dan reached over to pluck up a piece of pizza and took three bites, nearly inhaling the food and chewing hard. It made her smile, seeing him enjoying the pizza so much. He polished off another piece quickly and then stood. "I should go. Let you two ladies get back to whatever you were watching on TV."

"Won't you stay?" Chelsea asked.

"I'm beat, sis."

"But you'll be missing out on *Miracle on 34th Street*."

He crinkled his nose. "Say no more, I'm outta here." He gave Chelsea a kiss on the cheek. "Thanks for pizza." Then he swung around to stare into Erin's eyes. "Walk me out?"

Erin rose from her seat. "Of course."

She followed behind him, noting his amazing backside. Dan was built solid but all his pieces were beautifully placed and she'd been privy to touching every inch of him. She wanted to do it again and again, but she couldn't think past the next month, because unless things changed drastically, which was highly unlikely, she'd be gone.

Dan took his soft suede jacket from the coat closet and put his arms through the sleeves. Straightening the collar, he walked to the front door. "You don't have to go outside. It's cold out there."

The wind howled just at the moment as if giving Dan's comment legitimacy. It was cold and late, but she wasn't planning on going home just yet. She was looking forward to watching the movie with Chelsea.

Dan wound his arms around Erin's waist, bringing her up against him, and she glanced behind her to see where Chelsea was. She was discreet enough to keep out of sight.

"I'll pick you up tomorrow at four," Dan said.

She nodded. "Thank you." She put her hands on the lapels of his fur-lined jacket and stared into his eyes, and a moment later his mouth came down on hers. The kiss brought warmth and tingles, but it ended far too soon. Was it because his sister was in the other room? Or was Dan finally realizing that she wanted more from him than he was willing to give? She was too tired to dwell.

"Good night, sweetness," he said, and he walked out the door. She watched him saunter to his car and then turn, giving her a look of longing and maybe regret, it was hard to tell. When he put up his hand she waved back and then closed the door.

She blinked several times, noting something different in Dan tonight. A knot formed in her stomach and once again her heart ached, even though having Dan's baby would've been beyond complicated and blown up her list of Never Do's while in Texas.

"Hey, you alright in there?" Chelsea asked, coming around the corner to face her.

"Yeah, I'm fine. Are you ready to finish the movie?"

"Are you?" Chelsea pinned her with a curious look.

She put on a smile. "Sure, I'm ready for a little holiday cheer."

"Happy Thanksgiving, Mom."

"Same to you, honey. Oh, we miss you dearly." Erin loved hearing the sweet lilt in her mother's voice. It was hard being separated from her family during the holidays. "Tell me you've got wonderful plans for Thanksgiving, sweetheart."

Wonderful? She didn't know how wonderful it'd be if her instincts were right and Dan was truly backing away from her. But her mom didn't know anything about Dan yet. And she felt guilty about that. "I think it'll be a nice day. Yesterday, I helped my friend Chelsea make pies and cookies at her house. Chelsea, her brother Dan, and I are all going over to the Texas Cattleman's Club for a Thanksgiving feast later this afternoon. Will and Faye will be there, and Will's new girlfriend too. I think it's going to be a large gathering."

"That sounds lovely, but next year, I hope we'll spend the holiday together."

"I'd like that. Remember, I'm going to see you right after the first of the year."

"That's right. Your dad and I can't wait."

"So where are you having dinner tonight?"

"Sonya and Adam Marino invited us over to their house. They're marvelous cooks as you know, and we always have a pleasant time with them."

"Pleasant?" She lowered her voice. "You mean until Dad gets grumpy with all of their grandchildren running around, getting underfoot."

"I heard that," her father chimed in.

"Your father's right here listening in, and they have five little ones," her mom answered.

She smiled. "Hi, Dad."

"Hi, sweetheart. And I'll have you know I love

children, but five under age five, gets a bit crazy. Even your mother admits that. Right, Eloise?"

"Well…now that you mention it, Chuck," she heard her mom say. "It's a bit chaotic at times. Not enough to stay away from our good friends though."

"You'll have a great time."

"We hope you do too," her father said. "Love you to pieces."

"Me too," she told them. "Have a great day and we'll talk soon."

After the phone call, Erin couldn't stop thinking about how much in love her parents were. Their love filtered down to her, making her feel special and honored and humbled all at the same time. She'd really been lucky having two great parents and she never begrudged them their retirement time together. It gave Erin some freedom to seek her own dreams.

At least she'd mentioned Dan to her parents, though in a way that wouldn't brook any inquisition. She didn't know what she'd tell them about Dan. She'd picked up this amazing guy one night at a saloon and they were having a month long fling?

No, that wouldn't wash.

So she'd kept them in the dark about a man she had come to love. A really great guy who'd been terribly hurt as a boy and sadly whose scars ran deep. Maybe too deep for her to break through.

Erin moved to the closet and perused her wardrobe. She hadn't done a lot of shopping in Texas, and now she was kicking herself about that. She had no clue how to dress for a Thanksgiving dinner at an elite club. Was it formal, semiformal or casual?

She made a quick call to Chelsea to get some advice on what to wear to a Cattleman's Club holiday shindig and after her conversation, Erin felt better about her choices.

She hung up the phone and showered, washed and styled her hair, leaving it down and using the curling iron to make big barrel curls. She gave her hair a fluff and looked in the mirror, satisfied with the results, and then walked to her closet and picked out the one little black dress in her closet, that worked for special occasions like this. She selected her jewelry, a single long strand of silver loops with matching earrings, and set it all out on her bed. Done.

The weather was chilly so she hadn't gone for a run this morning, but now she wished she had. She had two hours to kill before Dan picked her up, so she donned her pink chenille robe, grabbed her iPad Mini and curled up on the chair near the fireplace to finish the mystery she'd started before she'd met Dan. She hadn't been sleeping well lately and soon her eyes grew heavy and she closed them, resting her head against the back of the chair.

Loud pounding startled her right out of the nice dream she was having. Her eyes opened and it took her a few seconds to finally get her bearings. "Oh no," she said, her head coming out of a fog.

The knocking now came with Dan calling her name. "Erin?"

She rose from the chair and walked over to the

door, yanking it open. "Dan, I'm so sorry. Have you been out there long?"

"A while," he said, taking in her robe and disheveled appearance.

Self-conscious, she tightened the lapels on her robe and stroked a hand through her hair. "I'm so sorry. I don't know what happened, I was reading and I must've dozed off."

"No problem," he said, stepping through the doorway. "There's no rush."

And she was finally able to gawk at him, dressed in crisp dark slacks and a silver-gray shirt covered by a black Western sports jacket, a black felt hat on his head and polished-to-a-shine snakeskin boots. "You look...yummy."

He grinned, eyeing the ties on her robe. "Get dressed, before I make us really late."

"Aye, aye," she said, saluting. "I'll be just a few minutes." Yet, a big fat thrill ran through her system at his suggestive comment.

She rushed into her bedroom, glad she had the foresight to pick out her clothes in advance. She slipped her robe off, put her bra on and turned around to pick up her dress. Dan called from behind the door, "You need help with the zipper, I'm on it."

She chuckled and a flash of heat rose up her throat. "I'll let you know."

She shimmied into her dress and reached up, reached down, and couldn't quite get to the middle of her back. Darn it. She really did need help with the long chic zipper doubling as an embellishment for the dress.

"Uh, Dan?"

The door opened and he faced her, her hands lifting her hair up and out of the way, and she turned around to give him access to the zipper. "Guess I do need help."

He came up behind her and she sniffed the very subtle, very masculine scent of his cologne. It was unique to him, probably something only rugged manly men wore, and it did things to her immediately.

Dan took his time zipping her up, inch by inch, careful with the lacy material, but he didn't touch any other part of her body, he didn't nibble on her throat, didn't kiss her at all, instead he backed away as soon as he was through. "There you go."

A sliver of disappointment wormed into her belly. Was it because they were running late? She was getting a weird vibe from him lately and it worried her.

"Thanks."

She slipped her feet into black heels and added the silver necklace she'd picked out.

"Do you have a coat?" he asked.

"I do." She grabbed her fur-trimmed coat, and slung her purse over her shoulder. "I'm ready."

"You look beautiful," he said.

He was saying all the right things, but...

"We should head out now. After you." He gestured with a sweep of his hand and she walked out of the cabin, Dan following behind.

* * *

As soon as Erin stepped foot inside the Cattleman's Club, she was in awe of the decorations. The entire place spoke of Thanksgiving. Autumn color wreaths decked with burnt orange, gold and purple leaves hung on the walls, plump ripe pumpkins sat on hay bales, fresh herbs flavored the air and overflowing cornucopia occupied the tables in the lobby area. As they walked farther inside, the waitstaff offered tumblers of mulled wine and Dan promptly grabbed two and handed her one.

She sipped gently, enjoying the new taste. They pressed on to the dining area, which was a whole new experience, from the golden candles casting the room in beautiful light to the fireplace crackling in cozy warmth. The tables were set with fresh autumn flower centerpieces and decorated with little touches adding to the holiday ambience. Christmas music played in the background.

"Wow, if the food's half as good as the decor, I'm gonna gain weight today."

Dan smiled. "It is. The staff prides themselves on their Thanksgiving meal. It's become a tradition at the club."

There were long tables as well as round tables, and they found Chelsea seated at one of the round tables with Will and Amberley and adorable Faye. Brandee was there too with her fiancé, Shane Delgado, and all of them rose as she and Dan approached. Being a part of their Thanksgiving dinner gave her a sense of belonging, a nice way to get to know some of them better.

Amberley held Faye, the baby still wearing a little overcoat, a bubbly pink hooded jacket that made her look exceedingly warm, especially in a room with the fireplace blasting. Will, Amberley and Chelsea each gave her a welcoming kiss on the cheek and introductions were made all around. She chose to sit between Will and Dan, with Chelsea on her brother's side. It was a lively group of people and as others filed in and took their seats, the room grew a bit noisy.

The event coordinator took the microphone at the head of the room. "Welcome everyone. It's our hope here at TCC that all of you will enjoy our abundant Thanksgiving feast and the fantastic desserts made by member Chelsea Hunt and guest Erin Sinclair."

All eyes turned to their table and a round of applause broke out. Erin loved being included, although it was totally unwarranted since Chelsea did all the hard work, yet she was grateful for the acknowledgment. She flashed Chelsea a big smile which was readily returned.

"So eat up everyone and from the staff and administration here at the Cattleman's Club, we wish you a wonderful Thanksgiving."

The room quieted after the announcement and finally Amberley looked at the baby. "Will, I think she's warm enough, she doesn't need the jacket anymore."

"Fine with me," he said, shrugging a shoulder and giving Erin a quick glance.

Hmm, something was up with him.

Amberley unzipped the baby's jacket and removed it down to the onesie the baby was wearing underneath and her eyes immediately teared up, her voice cracking. "Oh, Will."

Everyone turned their attention to the scene, as Amberley's hands began to shake and Will quickly took the baby from her. As he turned the baby onto his lap, everyone was privy to the message printed on Faye's onesie. "Amberley, will you marry my daddy please and be my new mommy?"

Will handed Faye to her. "Watch her a second for me, Erin."

"Certainly," she replied, and Faye fell into her arms and cuddled her neck. Immediately Erin began bouncing the baby on her lap.

Will rose from his seat and then got down on one knee, now garnering the attention of many in the dining room. "Amberley, I love you with all my heart and will until the end of time. Please be my wife, and mother to Faye. We both love you."

He opened a box and presented Amberley with a sparkling diamond ring.

Amberley was nodding her head, tears streaming down her face. "Yes. Yes."

Will placed the ring on her left hand and then rose, taking her along with him, and kissed her for all he was worth, for all the club to see.

Erin's eyes misted up as she rocked the baby. She

gave Dan a glance, her heart so open, so ready for this kind of love.

Dan could barely meet her eyes, his filling with regret and a stony resolve that almost sported a frown. He watched her holding Faye, bouncing her, snuggling her up tight and then he glanced away, staring off at some obscure point in the room.

The room exploded in oohs and aahs and a big round of applause. Everyone at the table rose to give Amberley and Will their congratulations. Dan also stood and put out his hand to Will. "Congratulations to both of you," he said. Dan always said the right thing, but Erin would never ever forget the look on his face as fear entered his eyes watching Erin's reaction to the whole scene.

The meal was served and joy abounded around the table for Amberley and Will. Despite Dan's sour mood, Erin couldn't contain her happiness. Little Faye would have a mother and father now to raise and love her, and what a wonderful thing that was. Soon talk of weddings dominated the conversation. Brandee was excited to explain the details to her own wedding plans to a very overwhelmed and thrilled Amberley. "And the reception is going to be in a converted barn on the ranch. We're doing it all up with lights and flowers."

"Sounds amazing," Erin said, finding her excitement contagious.

A moment later, Dan excused himself to get some air and Chelsea gave her a sympathetic look and shrugged.

Erin bit back sweeping sadness, vowing not to allow Dan to ruin her festive mood. But it clung to her anyway, like a spider's web that couldn't be pulled free. She had so little time left with Dan. Would she be able to go another month like this, loving him and not having it returned?

Chelsea slid over to Dan's seat. She gave her a smile and whispered, "Don't give up on him."

Had Chelsea read her thoughts?

"I...won't."

"Good," Chelsea said.

"I'm thrilled for Will and Faye. They both deserve happiness."

"So do you, Erin." Chelsea squeezed her hand.

Dan returned, his face more composed, his eyes unreadable, and Chelsea slid back to her seat and he sat down just as the trays of desserts were being brought around.

"Now you get to try some of everything," Erin said in good cheer, trying to ignore what was happening between them, the sense of dread curling her stomach right then.

Dan nodded, but his eyes were downcast, laden with regret. "I'm sorry, Erin."

She didn't ask for what. She knew why he was sorry. He couldn't, wouldn't, be making any kind of commitment to her. She shouldn't have gotten so heavily involved with him. The heartache wouldn't be worth the memories and she'd been foolish to think she could go into this situation lightly.

And when offered, neither one of them had the stomach to try any of the desserts.

Nine

Usually Dan liked being quiet. Usually he was fine being in his own head, but as he drove Erin home from the Thanksgiving meal, he was finding *her* silence a bit too much to bear. What he'd hoped would be a fun, enjoyable time for Erin at the Texas Cattleman's Club Thanksgiving feast, had turned out to be nothing of the kind.

Erin wasn't happy. He'd disappointed her and unintentionally hurt her in the process. Dan hated that. He'd never been so damn outright conflicted about a woman. He cared for Erin, a great deal, but he couldn't give her what she wanted. The delight he'd seen in her eyes at Will's unique and spontaneous way of proposing to Amberley, how lovingly she'd bounced and cuddled baby Faye in her arms, how she absorbed all talk of weddings and a hope-filled future, was like a mental slap to his face, telling him to wake up.

As he headed for her home, he gave Erin a glance just as she turned to him with those big gorgeous aqua eyes. Her smile though was sort of sad, or was he reading too much into all of this?

He pulled up to the cottage and parked the car. Erin was already getting out and he rushed around the hood to offer his hand. "Thanks," she said sweetly.

Her hand slipped into his and joy instantly filled his heart. The profound feeling overwhelmed him for a moment and he inhaled sharp and deep. He wasn't ready to let her go, they had another month together. She meant something to him. Something important and he didn't know what to do about it. He wasn't good with commitment and that wasn't about to change. This time of year especially firmed up his feelings on the subject. His mother's walking out on her family right before Christmas and all that had transpired after that, sealed the deal for him.

Erin wasn't a damsel in distress and he certainly wasn't Prince Charming in any way, shape or form. He didn't buy into the happily-ever-after scenario. He'd been scarred, for life.

He took her arm and walked her to the door. She turned her back to him and put the key in the lock. When she spun around, something flashed in her eyes and he was struck by momentary fear. *Of her leaving. Of her staying.*

Man, was he screwed up.

"Erin," he began.

"Shush," she said, her two fingers covering his lips. "Dan, don't say anything."

And then on tiptoes, she replaced her fingers with her mouth. The kiss startled him, heated him and made him want.

"Just come inside," she whispered.

Dan was hopeless to deny her anything, to deny himself more time with this amazing woman. "Sure thing, sweetness," he said, wrapping his arms around her and kissing her until she was breathless. Taking her hand, he led her straight into the bedroom.

Where neither one of them had to say anything more. Where moans and whimpers would be their only forms of communication.

Monday morning, Erin clocked herself at jogging four and a half miles and entered her cottage somewhat exhausted and sweating. She headed for a nice warm shower, reminding herself that November was coming to a quick close. Over the weekend, Erin did some Black Friday shopping with Chelsea. What she didn't find at the stores, she found online over the past few days and took advantage of free shipping from sites that desperately wanted her business. She'd taken long morning runs around the Flying E and spent most of her nights with Dan. He wasn't the same man she'd met at the Dark Horse Saloon. He was more cautious in what he said, more polite and much more determined to keep them from growing closer, to keep a divide between them. The gap was growing larger every day, but the nights were flaming hot. She couldn't quite merge the two in her mind. Obviously, Dan could. He'd showed his passion in every kiss, every touch, every way he made love to her, but then morning would roll around and he'd go back to being aloof and distant, while still being kind and generous.

It was that kindness and generosity that gave her a bit of hope, but was she fooling herself? Was she seeking out something, anything to cling to so she wouldn't have to do what her head was telling her to do? Break it off. Say goodbye. Sooner, rather than later.

But it wasn't only about Dan. She'd promised Will she'd stay through the holidays and she didn't want to miss being with Faye for her first Christmas. The Everetts, who were away for a few weeks, had made sure she knew she could stay as long as she liked in the guest cottage. Besides she didn't have anyone to go home to in Seattle. Her friends, the people she cared about were here.

Her phone rang just as she was drying off. She wrapped herself in the towel and picked up on the fourth ring. "I was beginning to think you weren't home," Dan said, his deep voice making her bones melt.

"Nope, just finishing up a shower after a long run."

"Need some help?"

"I think I got this, Hunt," she said. Dan was an expert at drying her up and then making her wet again. "What's up?"

"Remember when I mentioned the possibility of Brentley Jamison being Maverick?"

"Yes," she said, sobering up. "The guy was a congressman's son, right?"

"I'm sorry to say he's not our guy."

"And how do you know for sure?"

"The police contacted Congressman Jamison and found out his son, Brentley, has been in a drug rehab in California for more than six months."

"But couldn't he still do some damage using a computer or something?"

"Guess not. He's pretty bad off. He doesn't have use of a computer and only approved visitors can see him. He's not our guy, Erin."

"Have you told Chelsea?"

"Yeah. She's disappointed. I guess I shouldn't have mentioned it without something more concrete to go on."

"Chelsea knows you're only trying to help her."

"Thanks for saying that."

"It's true. Chelsea knows you have her back. She appreciates everything you've been trying to do to find the pervert."

"It's frustrating."

"Yeah, life can be like that sometimes."

"So what are you doing tonight?"

"Tonight? I have a hot date with a handsome guy and his two girls."

Dan paused for a moment. "Oh yeah, that's right. You're having dinner with Will."

"And Amberley and Faye," she added.

"Have a good time."

"It should be fun. I miss that little munchkin. And, Dan, thanks for keeping me in the loop with the investigation."

"Sure thing."

She was about to ask him to come over afterward, but held back. She didn't want to seem needy or desperate. Not even the suggestive banter at the beginning of the conversation meant he'd subject her to a late night booty call. That was Dan, being decent and kind. And why she was so much in love with him.

"I'll see you tomorrow night, sweetness. I'll bring dinner."

"Can you bring Lucky too? I miss him."

"Babies and dogs, a guy could get jealous."

If only.

Just minutes later the phone rang again. Erin looked at the screen and then blinked a few times, before picking up. "Hello, Mrs. Lawrence."

"How are you, Erin?"

"I'm doing well."

"That's good to hear. I'm afraid there's a situation that involves your upcoming job. I know this is very last-minute but we're in a bit of a predicament."

"What is it?" Her heart began to pound. Was she going to lose her job, before she'd even been given a chance? A myriad of emotions ran through her body, the most being panic that she could face unemployment again. A terrible prospect. But if she did, she could stay on in Texas and find work here.

"I'm afraid that the musical director you're replacing went into labor last night, seven weeks early."

"Oh my goodness." This, she didn't expect. "How is she doing?"

"Jody had a baby boy at four this morning. Baby and mom are fine, thankfully, although the baby will need expert care to catch him up to speed. He's a tiny one, but he's doing well under the circumstances as I understand."

"That's a relief," she said, glad for mother and baby. How scary that must've been for the family. But Erin was smart enough to know what was coming next and her stomach began to ache.

"As you might expect, this puts us in a precarious spot. We have no one here to head our winter spectacular and the kids are so looking forward to it. Jody has had them working on the songs and the parents are making costumes. So my question to you is this, would you possibly consider moving up your hire date to first thing next week? That would give you a full week to work with the kids before the performance. I realize it might be difficult or impossible for you to get away so quickly, but we're hoping for a miracle here."

A miracle? Certainly, she couldn't produce a miracle of any kind, but the more she thought about it, the more sense it began to make. She didn't want to disappoint the kids at her school for one. She didn't want to let down the staff at Lincoln Elementary, either, they'd been so generous in offering her the position, basically sight unseen. And mostly, it would solve her dilemma about Dan. She would have to leave Texas eventually and going to work earlier than expected was one kind of solution. She'd be heartbroken, but it might be smarter to leave now, than after another month of seeing him. It had to be better all around to make a swift, clean break. What reason did she have to stay in Texas anyway when she was so sorely needed in Seattle?

She didn't have a rational reason to refuse. At least this way she'd go, knowing she was needed and wanted. She couldn't disappoint the kids. "Miracles happen. At least this one will. I'll come as soon as I can get a flight out. I'll contact you when I arrive back in Seattle."

"Really?" Immense joy sounded in the older woman's voice. "You'll come to work a month early? Oh, I can't tell you what this means to me, the school and the kids. And don't be surprised if we roll out the red carpet for you, you're our hero. I can't thank you enough."

"No red carpet necessary. I'm only too glad to help. I had no real plans for the holiday anyway."

"And now you do."

"Yes," she said. It was a bittersweet situation. "Now I do."

The next day, Erin jogged past the guest cabins on the Flying E, the main house and the livestock that had become a regular sight to her on her morning runs. This was her last full day here, the last time she'd run these paths, the last time she'd breathe in crisp Texas air as she worked her body to the max, feeling the strain of her muscles, the pull of her limbs. She was exhausting herself deliberately, so she'd think about the pain racking her body rather than the pain tormenting her heart.

It was working too, and she slowed her pace to catch her breath. The sky overhead was crystal clear today, not a cloud to be found. The golden sun was shining but the air had a bite to it and she relished the cooler temps calming her revved up body.

Last night, she said her goodbyes to Amberley, Will and Faye. They vowed to keep in touch no matter what, and made her promise to come to their wedding. She was swarmed with hugs and good wishes at her new position in Seattle, one Will had a hand in helping her attain, and she left them feeling better about her decision, feeling loved.

By the time she got to her cabin, she was walking at a snail's pace, feeling drained of energy. "You are ridiculous, Erin." Running until she was ready to drop didn't solve anything. She still had to muster up her courage and tell Dan her news when he stopped over tonight. She was not looking forward to it, not looking forward to the demise of the most wonderful month she'd ever spent in her life.

She shed her clothes and showered. The hard beads of hot water revitalized her somewhat, and she toweled off and stepped into fresh clothes. She combed through her hair and padded to the closet to pull out her suitcases. Just the sight of them on her bed made her breath catch. Robotically, she began to fill them up, and with each garment she placed inside the darkly lined interior, memories flooded her mind. She folded her now-infamous outfit she wore for the bucking bull night at the Dark Horse Saloon and placed it inside. It was where she'd met Dan and they'd saved Lucky. She fingered the blouse she'd worn, smiling sadly.

Next, her horseback-riding-with-Dan pants were placed on top. Beside it she put in her luncheon-with-Chelsea outfit and then added her sexy lingerie. She didn't even want to think about those heated nights with her Texan, her heart was aching enough. Her memories would be locked inside her head for eternity. Boots and other accessories filled another small suitcase and, except for the last-minute things she'd need tomorrow morning for the flight home, she was fully packed.

Thanking Clay and Sophie Everett for letting her stay at his beautiful ranch was next on her list, but the Everetts were still out of town, so she sat down on the sofa, pen and paper in hand, crossed her legs and put a thick *Cowboys and Indians* magazine underneath the paper to compose her thank-you note.

She was very grateful to everyone associated with the Flying E Ranch. They'd welcomed her with open arms, making sure she was comfortable in the cottage/cabin she'd called home for this month. A girl could get used to…

Tears filled her eyes as she penned her letter of thanks and when she was through, she realized how very much this place meant to her. In a sense she'd become a different woman here, someone who took stock in her own capabilities, someone who'd ventured out to take risks and had grown into a stronger person for it. She'd learned to love again too, the real kind of love, not just some whimsical fascination with a man, but to feel deeply inside and know what beamed brightly inside her was true and honest.

Yes, she could look at Dan and say this time with him had been eye-popping. She'd fallen in love and also helped with an investigation. Both had given her joy, but right now, both were ending in disappointment. At least for her.

She sealed the letter to Clay, closing one more door to Texas.

She spent the rest of the afternoon, straightening out the place, putting things back in order. Her mother always told her to leave a place better than when she'd arrived. Well, the cabin was perfect in her estimation, but she did find some wildflowers growing outside and filled a vase and placed it on top of the mantel.

She lit candles in cinnamon and apple fragrances that filled the entire cabin with the spirit of the holiday season. And she baked a quick batch of ready-made cookies. The mingling of scents wafted in the air. The only thing missing was a crackling fire in the fireplace, but she didn't have the heart to go that far.

By five o'clock, the sun was falling into the sky, leaving a dim, murky coolness behind. She was dressed in her favorite outfit, a bulky cream sweater and long black skirt. She wore boots and bustled around the kitchen, until the knock came at the door.

She heard the rumblings of Lucky, his tail swishing against the door, his whimpers in anticipation of being let inside. It made her smile. In that moment, quickly and without regret, she made a decision. It was probably the hardest decision of her life, but if she'd learned one thing by being there in Texas, it was to be strong, and do what you deemed was right. She'd been hiding behind her recent bad relationship too long.

It wasn't going to be easy and if the moment wasn't right, she may very well back out, but at least she had determination on her side. And a sense of clearing the air.

She opened the door and Lucky immediately lunged for her, nearly knocking her down. She stepped back and found her balance, the dog's front paws on her tummy.

"Lucky, down," Dan commanded.

"No, it's okay, Dan. I missed him too."

She hugged Lucky, kissing the very top of his head and ruffling his fur. "You're a good, good boy," she cooed, in her baby Faye voice.

Dan entered the house, his arms loaded with covered dishes of food, and walked into the kitchen to set everything down. "Dinner," he announced.

"Thanks," Erin said, the dog underfoot as she

closed the front door. "Smells wonderful." Not that she had an appetite. She really didn't. She had a lot to say to Dan and her throat was ready to close up any second.

"It's brisket and corn soufflé and creamed spinach. From Hunt and Company Steakhouses. It's one of our signature meals. It was time you tried it."

She sidled up next to him and he turned to give her a kiss on the cheek.

She gave him a small smile, her heart heavy. "I guess it is."

"One of these days, we'll go to my best restaurant in Dallas and enjoy a quiet candlelit meal."

She was going into Dallas tomorrow. Dallas Fort Worth Airport, to be exact. Will had given her an open-ended ticket when they'd first arrived. She never thought she'd be leaving without him and Faye but fate had been on his side.

Unlike with her.

Dan began opening the covered dishes. "Are you ready to eat, sweetness? I'm kinda starving. Missed lunch today."

"Sure, we can sit down and eat."

She was rescued, given a bit of a respite from having to tell Dan she was leaving. They went about putting plates on the table, filling glasses of iced tea and dishing up the food. It was uncanny how efficiently they worked together in the kitchen. And it was hard to think this was going to be the last time.

Once everything was set out, Dan pulled the chair

out for her, always the gentleman. She took her seat and glanced at the food.

"You first," he said.

She put a sparse amount of food on her plate. Everything truly did smell delicious and to be polite, she would eat some of it. Dan filled his plate, growled about digging in and he began eating. Every so often, he would give Lucky a taste and the happy boy's tail swished back and forth like an out of control metronome. It was such a simple thing, but so sweet to see Lucky at Dan's heels.

She nibbled on her meal and sipped her iced tea.

"I made cookies," she said after the meal was finished. "Would you like dessert now?"

He leaned way back in the chair and patted his firm-as-granite belly. "Can we wait a bit? I practically inhaled the meal and can't think about eating another bite."

"Sure."

"Want a fire?" he asked.

"Uh, no." She didn't think she could sit by the fire with him tonight.

"What's up? You're pretty quiet tonight."

"Actually, can we go sit in the parlor? I have something to tell you."

His eyes pinned to hers, and he gave her a nod. "Sure thing."

He waited for her to rise and took her hand. She squeezed her eyes closed, absorbing his touch, the way he took control and led her to the sofa. Lucky wasn't far behind. She sat and Dan sat beside her.

Lucky roamed the room and then after circling an area a few times, found a comfy spot on the rug and nestled down.

In typical Dan style, he didn't say a thing. He simply waited for her to speak. So this had to be it. She couldn't procrastinate, she couldn't stall any longer. All the words she'd practiced in her head didn't come when she finally opened her mouth. "I, uh, I've been called in to work earlier than expected. The woman I was replacing at the school went into premature labor. I don't have much choice. They really need me."

Dan began nodding his head, watching her carefully. "How soon?"

"My flight leaves tomorrow."

"Tomorrow? Oh man," he said, running his hands down his face. "That soon?"

"Yeah, that soon." She spoke quietly. "I didn't expect this."

"No, I didn't, either. They can't do without you for a few more weeks?"

"No, they have no one else to fill in. And since they hired me, I'm sort of obligated to go. There's this winter concert the children have been working on all semester. I can't disappoint the students."

"But you can disappoint me?" He gave her a look, his eyes pinning her down.

"I don't want to disappoint anyone, Dan. We both knew this day would eventually come. I'm just… leaving sooner than we expected. I really don't want to go."

At all. But she couldn't tell him that. She couldn't reveal how breaking up with him, was also killing her inside. That she still held a shred of hope that there'd be a Hollywood ending, where he took her by the hand, kissed her senseless and told her not to leave him. Ever.

"So this is it." It wasn't a question, but a declaration. To his credit, he hung his head and sat immobilized in his seat. The air was still, Lucky's breathing the only sound in the room.

She hated to say the words that would end it, so she held her tongue and waited.

After a few moments, he spoke. "Erin, it's a rare thing to be able to work in a field you love. And it's a great opportunity for you. Once I heard you play, I realized music has to be in your life."

She nodded, hiding her grief. She could argue that music was always in her life. And that she could teach music anywhere, not just in Seattle.

She had to lay her cards on the line. Dan had to know her feelings, even if she didn't come right out and say those three little words. "Dan, this past month has been wonderful. I want you to know, I don't look at my time with you as a casual fling. Being w-with you, meant s-something special to me. *You* mean something special to me."

"You mean something special to me too, sweetness." Dan covered her hand and tugged her close. His lips came down on hers and his kiss drew her into a mix of mind-blowing pleasure and unfair torture. She loved him. She didn't have the courage to tell him, but he had to know, to see how she gave him everything she had to give, to feel the way she responded to him.

Unable to stand it another second, she pulled away from him. "Sorry," she said, holding back tears. "This is hard."

"For me too."

Dan pushed his hands through his hair. "Let me take you to the airport tomorrow."

"No." She didn't have to think twice about it. A tearful public goodbye at the airport would be too difficult and quite possibly humiliating. "But thank you for offering."

"You're sure?"

"Yes. I'm sure." She gulped air.

"Okay."

And they sat there on the sofa for long moments quietly, Dan taking her back in his arms and holding her tight. It felt so right, but obviously Dan didn't seem to think it right enough.

"I can stay a little longer, if you'd like," he whispered. "Unless you have packing to do."

She took half a second to think about it. She never wanted him to leave, but she mustered her courage, aware that the longer he stayed, the harder it would be. "I have some things to do," she said diplomatically. It was a bold-faced lie, but necessary for her sanity.

"Then I'd better go."

She gave a slight nod. Staring into his handsome face, she committed it to memory and tried not to tear up. She would probably never see Dan again. Once they parted, they would walk separate paths, as if they'd never met. As if this short time was merely a blip in their lifetimes. How terribly sad.

He rose from the sofa, a deep sigh pushing out of his chest. The sound resonated and her sorrow was almost tangible. He reached for her and arm in arm they walked to the door. "I'll miss you, sweetness," he said, turning to face her as he put his jacket on.

"Dan," she began, but the words choked in her throat.

He enveloped her into his arms, giving her a big bear hug. Her beast of a man was leaving, exiting her life. Even though, she was the one going, it felt the other way around. He hadn't asked her to stay. He hadn't declared his love. He wouldn't and it was a hard pill to swallow.

As he bent his head and claimed her mouth in another tantalizing kiss, she gripped the lapels of his jacket and gave him a kiss back that he would hopefully never forget. When they finally broke apart, she felt the loss down to her toes.

"Call me if you change your mind about the airport," he whispered.

She wouldn't. "Okay, but I don't think so."

"Safe travels, sweetness," he said.

And then with Lucky by his side, he stepped out into the cold evening and walked down the path that led to his car. Halfway there, he stopped dead in his tracks, dipping his head as if eyeballing the ground.

A few seconds passed. Her heart pounded, wondering what he was thinking, what he was doing.

And then he sighed heavily, lifted his head and resumed walking to his car. It was painful seeing him go, ending it this way. Her hopes died then and as he opened the car door, he looked her way and waved, his beautiful face partly hidden in the shadows of night.

She waved back, giving him a last smile.

It was over.

She closed the door and amazingly didn't fall apart watching Dan drive away. No, she'd save that for later tonight. Right now, she had something else to do.

She picked up her cell and called her new friend. The call went straight to voice mail and Erin was once again disappointed. Maybe she shouldn't have waited to tell Chelsea her plans, but she had to tell Dan first before she told his sister about her departure. "Chelsea, hi. It's me, Erin. I'm sorry I didn't reach you. Please call me when you get in. I have something important to tell you."

She'd stop by Chelsea's first thing in the morning to say her goodbyes.

It would be her last heartbreaking order of Texas business, before she boarded the plane headed for Seattle.

Ten

Erin's fingers flew across the piano keys and she nodded her head for the fifth grade class to start singing a rendition of "Winter Wonderland." The lively sounds filled her music room, most of the children singing in the right key and, all in all, their voices blending well in a song perfect for the oldest kids in the school. These children would graduate in less than six months and head off to middle school.

When the song ended, she stood from the piano bench and applauded. "That was wonderful, class." Their singing sounded better than her piano playing. She was rusty, and had come to the school the day after she'd arrived to do some informal practice. It gave her something solid to do, and boy, she really had needed the quality time at the piano.

"Next, let's practice 'Happy to All.'"

She sat down again, gave the class their cue and began playing. The children's eyes were beaming; they were glad to be out of regular class and spending an hour doing something fun. It was no different when she was in school, only she'd had a true love of music, so coming to music class wasn't only about getting out of academics, it was about her passion.

She wanted to say she felt fulfilled at Lincoln Elementary. She wanted to say, taking this position working with music and children, her two true loves, was her everything. She was new to the school and the faculty here. She vowed to give herself some time to adjust. But right now, the wholeness she once felt teaching music wasn't there.

Her heart was still in Texas. With Dan.

She played the final note on the piano and rose again. "That was pretty good, class. But it needs a bit of work. Some of you aren't remembering the words." She grabbed a pile of printouts of the song. "Here you go," she said, passing them out. "Take this home, study the lyrics and practice it with your parents tonight."

A series of groans followed. "Hey, it's not so bad. It's a fun kind of homework," she said. "I'll see you all tomorrow. Have a good rest of the day."

After she dismissed the class, she found Shelly at the door, smiling. "That was a great practice," she said, stepping into the room. "I came by to see if there's anything else you might need? Anything we can do for you?"

"Hi, Shelly." She glanced around the classroom, the

stepped rows and the shelves of musical instruments. Later on today, the fourth graders would practice ringing the bells. "No, I can't think of anything right now."

"So, your first official day is going well?"

"I think so," she said, giving her a smile.

"Great. Well, it's lunchtime. Shall we go grab a bite?"

"Yes."

After she closed up the music room, she walked with Shelly toward the teachers' lounge. As soon as the principal opened the door, Erin was hit with a barrage of twenty staff members all smiling and waiting for her and applauding as she stepped inside. Construction paper signs on the windows exclaimed, Welcome to Lincoln! Many Thanks!

Food was set out on decorated tablecloths, an abundance of salads and sandwiches and desserts.

"I hope this isn't too overwhelming," Shelly whispered in her ear. "The staff sometimes gets carried away. You saved our butts, and we wanted to throw you a welcome party."

"Oh, this is so…" Words escaped her. She *was* overwhelmed. And grateful. "It's really lovely."

And it was. Over lunch, she spent time meeting many of the teachers and staff working at the school. It gave her a sense of balance and perspective. She got an earful about school politics, rules and which parents to watch out for. That last one made her laugh. She'd had run-ins with helicopter parents before, their hovering and over-involvement bordering on obnoxious at times. But she'd met some really amazing parents too, and so it all equaled out.

Erin made a point of thanking everyone for their gracious welcome to the school and when lunch was over, she began walking back to her music room. Her phone dinged. She stopped to read the text coming up from the screen. It was Dan.

How's your first day going? he asked.

It was his third text to her since she'd been back. The first one simply was to make sure she'd made it safely back to Seattle. It wasn't much more than a friendly gesture.

The second one was a one-liner wishing her good luck on her first day on the job. She'd answered him with a short reply.

And now today. She needed a clean break from him. He had no idea how much hearing from him like this was hurting her. No phone calls. No "I'm miserable without you"s. He was trying to be her text buddy. Well, she didn't want his friendship. Or rather, she did but only if that friendship came with more.

She tucked her phone back into her sweater pocket without texting him back. She had to get ready for the fourth graders and the bells. Dan was a distraction she didn't need right now. He'd muddled up her mind and broken her heart enough for one lifetime. She was still raw from missing him, still at odds with his unwillingness to let go of his past. Still sorta mad at him for being dense. She supposed she was going through the stages of breakup grief all at once. Whatever it was, it was painful in a way that she'd never experienced before. She hated that she'd cried herself to sleep for the past few nights.

By the end of the school day, she had chucked away her first-day jitters. That at least was a positive thing. She'd made it through and it wasn't terrible. In fact, the day went smoothly enough and the welcome party was an added surprise. She could feel good about all of that.

As she got into her car, a few of the teachers waved to her in the parking lot and she smiled and waved back. They were nothing if not really friendly and she was lucky to be a part of this school.

But, even with spending the entire day singing fun winter songs, teaching the younger ones the words and playing tunes on the piano, she wasn't in much of a festive mood.

Hours later, Erin sat on her bed in her tiny studio apartment eating almond chicken and noodles she'd picked up from China East, her favorite restaurant. It was dark in the city, the gloomy Seattle weather casting shadows earlier than usual. She was already cozy in her jammies and ready to turn on the television when her cell phone rang.

Immediately, she conjured up an image of Dan and her heart thumped hard in her chest.

Setting her food aside, she picked up the phone and didn't immediately recognize the number. "Hello."

"Hello, Erin. This is Rex. Don't hang up the phone, please."

Her stomach churned. Just the sound of his voice

brought back bad memories. "Why are you calling me?"

"I need to speak to you. It's important."

She had a mind to shut him down, turn off her phone and go about her business, but curiosity was a funny thing. "You have two minutes. Go."

"Dan's been mopey all week," Darla said to Chelsea as soon as she stepped foot inside his house at Hunt Acres.

"Have not," Dan said, in earshot range of the exchange by the front door.

"Well, I'll cheer him up." Chelsea walked farther into the house. "I brought your share of Christmas ornaments. Do you have mine?"

"Somewhere," Dan said. He had no idea where he'd stashed them from last year. Decorating the Christmas tree was the last thing on his mind. He'd been thinking about Erin 24/7 and it was affecting his work, his free time and his life in general. She wasn't always prompt in returning his texts. In fact, his last two to her had gone unanswered. Was she okay? Had she forgotten about him so quickly? No, that wasn't fair. He hadn't given her a reason not to forget about him.

"Such a nice tradition, trading your family's ornaments with each other every year," Darla said.

"We've been rotating them since Dad passed," Chelsea said. "But you're not getting these, big brother, until I get yours."

Darla shot Chelsea a smug look. "I know where

they've been tucked away in the garage. I'll go grab them for you."

"Do you need any help?" Chelsea asked.

"Nope, I can manage just fine," she said. "Let me take those off your hands." Darla took the box out of Chelsea's arms. "I'll put them in the spot the tree will go. Hint. Hint. Maybe it'll get you in the holiday spirit," she said and then walked out of the room.

Chelsea followed him into the kitchen and he poured them each a cup of coffee. "Here," he said, handing her a mug. Steam rose up and the strong scent flavored the air. "There are some of Darla's biscuits in the fridge. You can heat one up."

"No, thanks, I've had breakfast, but I might take one to go."

"I hear there's been a break in the case. It couldn't have happened soon enough. What can you tell me?" Dan asked.

"Yeah, well, it is good news. The authorities have a beat on who Maverick is and they're working on it night and day. Apparently, he wasn't so clever not to leave behind a clue. They found a digital footprint on the hard drive discovered in Adam Haskell's car that has led them to break open the case. We should know soon who Maverick is."

"Amen to that," Dan said. "I'd like to see justice done to that guy, in the worst way." He leaned against the counter and took a gulp of coffee.

"Until this guy is behind bars, I won't have closure. I'll never get over the violation, but it'll help knowing the criminal got his due."

He couldn't agree more. At least that was one good thing happening in his life lately.

"Dan," Chelsea said, a sisterly pout on her lips. "You look…miserable. Like you need a giant hug or something."

He rolled his eyes. He'd been avoiding Chelsea this week. His sister's heart was in the right place, but she was also a big pain. Ever since Erin left town, Chelsea had been calling or texting him every day *to see how he was doing.*

As if he couldn't live without Erin.

As if he was in some sort of pain or something.

As if his total lack of concentration had something to do with her leaving town.

"I don't need—"

She wouldn't let get him get the words out. Soon, he found himself wrapped in her arms, and she was giving him consolatory pats on the back. "I know it's hard," she said.

His teeth gnashed. "Sis…shut the eff up, okay?"

"Wow. I didn't know it was that bad."

"Nothing's bad." She could be exasperating at times.

"You let that girl walk out of your life."

"I didn't send her packing. She got a job. A good job."

"Did you ask her to stay?"

"No, and you know why I didn't, so don't pretend innocence on this. I don't do long-term relationships."

"Because you've never met the right woman. Erin wasn't just some girl you were dating. She was your soul mate. She understood you. She made you happy."

"Yeah, the way Mom made Dad happy?"

"Dan, honestly." She chewed her lower lip and gave her head a shake. "Mom never loved Dad. Not in the way that counts. She didn't return the love he'd given her. You can't keep comparing every woman to Mom, especially Erin. You know her heart. You know she's a good person."

"You bake cookies with her one day and suddenly you're an expert on Erin Sinclair."

"We've gotten closer than that. I consider her my friend. She's confided in me and normally I wouldn't betray that confidence, but you need to hear this. She didn't want to leave Texas. Or you. She told me she'd fallen for you."

Dan winced. It was hard enough speaking about Erin with his sis, but to hear her say how much Erin cared, cut a path straight to his heart.

"When was the last time you spoke to her?"

Dan frowned. "She didn't answer my last text."

"Are you telling me you haven't spoken to her, you know, using real words over the phone, since she left? You're just texting her?"

"Yeah, that's right."

"Oh brother," she said, mocking him, saying without saying, he was a real jerk. "Okay, so then, you don't know what's going on with her."

Dan's head snapped up. "What's going on with her? Did you talk to her?"

"Yes, we actually *speak* on the phone," Chelsea said snarkily. "I talked to her last night."

"And?"

Dan's heart began to pound. *Crap.* He wasn't enjoying this conversation. If something was up with Erin, he wanted to know.

"Tell me, Chels." His voice came out more like a plea than a command. He hated giving his little sis that much satisfaction, but he'd been grouchy ever since Erin cut him off by not returning his text. He'd never felt a loss so great as he had this past week.

"Nothing," Chelsea said, "except that her ex, that Rex guy, is sniffing around again. He's broken it off with his wife for good and wants Erin back. Bigtime, from what I understand."

"She wouldn't go back to him," he snapped. "That guy's a real jerk."

Chelsea didn't say anything, only shrugged her shoulders.

"What does that mean?" he asked, his blood quickly coming to a boil.

"It means, all I know is Erin is lonely and hurt and missing you. She's vulnerable right now and when women get that way sometimes they do stupid things."

Dan started pacing the floor, shaking his head.

"But since you don't care… I mean you've pretty much written her off…"

Dan glared at Chelsea. "I do care, damn it. I love her. I love Erin, okay? Nothing's been right since she left."

Immediately, Chelsea's face softened and she smiled.

Dan too felt a softening and a heavy weight being lifted from his shoulders. He loved Erin, probably fell in love with her the second she'd bravely hoisted herself up on that mechanical bull, only he'd been so entrenched in his own resolve not to let any woman hurt him that he'd suppressed those feelings.

He'd been a fool and had pushed away someone who deserved only 100 percent from the man she loved. That man *had* to be him. He was through fighting it. His heart was open now and he vowed to give Erin Sinclair everything he had to give. He only hoped it was enough.

"Dan," Chelsea said, her voice gentle, her smile encouraging. "Don't tell me. Tell her."

"Right," he agreed. Chelsea just might've been shocked at his quick turnaround. "And thanks for not gloating."

"Me?" She pointed to herself. "I wouldn't do that. I'm happy for you, Dan. Erin's perfect for you. Don't lose her."

"I won't. I promise."

He glanced at his watch. "I gotta go. Have things to do, people to see." He gave Chelsea a quick kiss on the cheek. "Thanks, sis, you're the best."

"You might not think so after I tell you this."

"Tell me what?"

Chelsea wrinkled her nose. "Erin listened to Rex for two minutes, then told him where to go and hung up on him."

He laughed. "That's my girl."

"You're not mad at me?"

"You're a sly one, but you sure do know how to get your point across and I'm too damn relieved to be mad at anyone right now."

* * *

Dan's nerves were about to split in half as he walked up the steps of Lincoln Elementary School. Distant music and children's singing reached his ears and all he had to do was follow the sounds to find the auditorium.

To find Erin.

He wore his suit for the occasion, a dark jacket over a crisp white shirt, boots and his Stetson planted firmly on his head. He carried a dozen ruby-red roses and inside his pocket was a tiny deep crimson box housing a three-carat diamond ring he hoped Erin would accept. He'd had Raina Patterson from Priceless help him design the ring and he'd put a rush on it. If anything was *priceless* it was Erin and he could only hope he wasn't too late. He'd made a mess of things and he was there to fix it. It helped knowing she'd kicked that Rex guy to the curb, but even if she hadn't, he would fight long and hard for her.

What a dope he'd been.

He stepped into the back of the filled-to-capacity auditorium, wintry snow-laden scenes on construction paper murals decorating the place. On rows of risers, a throng of kids with happy faces and beaming eyes sang their hearts out. The winter concert was in full swing.

His gaze drifted left to the woman gracefully sweeping across the piano keys, making the performance all come together.

His heartbeat sped at the sight of her and he drew deep breaths. God, he hadn't realized until this minute how much he'd missed her. Dressed in a gray-

and-snowy-white sweater with a knit cap on her head, she was the best sight he'd ever seen.

She nodded her head and gave the kids their cues, and Dan waited and watched patiently for the performance to end. Class after class came up on stage, looking to Erin for guidance. It seemed like an eternity and finally the performance was over, the risers emptied and the school principal came up to say a few words into the mike.

"Everyone, let's give a big hand to Miss Sinclair for making our Winter Wonderland Concert a huge success. She saved the day and did a fantastic job, don't you agree?"

Erin rose from the piano, waved at the crowd and was met with a round of applause.

Immediately Dan marched down the aisle to face Erin at the front of the auditorium. "She saved me too," Dan said loud enough for the entire room to hear.

Her legs nearly buckled when she saw him and her face registered surprise. "Dan?"

"Hi, sweetness," he said and then bounded up the few steps to the stage. He walked over to her and laid the bouquet into her arms. "For you."

She glanced at the audience—who were now kind of mesmerized by the scene—and then she turned her pretty blue-green eyes to him. "What're you doing here?"

"I came to take my girl home, to Texas."

He removed his hat, dug into his pocket and there before the entire room of children and parents and staff

of Lincoln Elementary, took a knee and presented her
the custom-made, only for her, glittering diamond ring.

The room erupted in oohs and aahs, and he got
the feeling everyone was glued to their seats.

Erin's eyes misted and he hoped that was a good
sign. "Oh, Dan."

"Erin Sinclair, I've missed you like crazy. I love
you beyond any words I could ever say, beyond any
lyrics ever written. I'm here, humbled and honored
to ask you to marry me. To be my wife. To take a
place beside me at Hunt Acres."

Tears streamed down Erin's face now, and she
began nodding her head, her body shaking, almost as
much as his was. She reached for him and he rose to
look at her beautiful face. "Yes, yes, I'll marry you."

Loud applause broke out around the room. Dan was
oblivious to the crowd now, Erin said yes and he quickly
took the ring and placed it on her left ring finger.

She stared at it and grinned, her tears flowing
freely. Happy tears.

Then she faced the people who witnessed it all,
lifting her left hand and wiggling her fingers. "I'm
engaged," she said, awe in her voice.

Dan used his Stetson to shield wandering eyes
and kissed her silly, grinning and giddy, showing her
how much she meant to him. Then he tugged her off
stage, the show over, but his life finally beginning.

"I still can't believe you did that," Erin said, hours
later. Dan, her dreamboat guy sat next to her on
the edge of her bed in her apartment. "You, Mr.

Quiet, who doesn't like to draw attention to himself, brought down the house."

"I did, didn't I?" Dan had a perpetual grin on his face and Erin wasn't too far from that, either.

"You laid out your heart to me, Dan. It was…the best proposal ever."

"I love you. I wanted to show you how much."

"You did," she said. "And I love you too."

"The rescuer became the rescued," he said, taking her hand and stroking over her fingers.

"How did I rescue you?"

"Don't you know?" he asked.

She shook her head, not sure what he was getting out.

"You taught me that it's okay to take a risk. To go for it. To do something out of your comfort zone. I was so set in my way of thinking, sure I'd never truly love anyone. I wouldn't allow myself to. And then you came along and I couldn't wrap my head around how much I not only wanted to be with you, but needed to be with you."

"Would've been nice if you'd told me all that."

"I know, and I'm sorry. I should've realized what you meant to me before you left. I should have stopped you from going. I took the coward's way out and I'm beating myself up about that now. But I'm also through with it, all of it. I want you. I love you and I'm at peace, sweetness."

"And why is that?"

"Because I've let it go. Because now I have you. I'm through dwelling in the past. And if I'm being totally honest with you, when you took that pregnancy test, yes, I was scared about it but there was a part of me that was really disappointed. I couldn't find my way to ask you to stay with me but if you were carrying my child…"

"You wouldn't have had a choice. We would've been permanently tied to each other."

"Yeah, and I think I wanted that. I was just afraid to admit it. I want babies with you, sweetness. As many as you want and as quickly as you want."

"Oh, Dan. Yes, I want to have your babies. Soon, real soon."

Dan smiled warmly and claimed her lips in a beautifully sweet kiss, and she closed her eyes, envisioning a future with him, a life of fullness and love and babies.

When the kiss ended, he continued to hold her hand, giving it a squeeze. "Chelsea had something to do with all this too. She can be a devil when she wants to be."

"Oh yeah? How do you mean?"

"She let it slip, intentionally, I'm sure, that your ex was trying to get you back. I, uh, kinda saw red then, hating the thought and realizing that it wasn't just Rex that I didn't want in your life, but any man other than me."

"That's sweet." She stroked his face. "So you faced facts. You loved me."

"Yeah."

"Couldn't live without me?"

"Yeah."

"Wanted to marry me?"

"Yeah." Dan smiled "And don't forget about Lucky. He's been in a funk since you left town."

"How I love that dog. So then, I'm glad Chelsea told you, but the truth is when Rex called me, I felt absolutely nothing for him. When he told me he'd left his wife and wanted me back, I laughed. Seriously laughed at him, and told him to get a life. Without me. I hung up the phone and that was that. I guess I made my point."

"You did. I knew you'd never take him back. You have better taste than that."

She smiled, her heart overflowing. "Yeah, I do. I picked you, didn't I? And I have a confession to make to you. I pretty much knew I wasn't going to stay on at Lincoln after the holidays. They'd been wonderful to me, but that was just it. As great as everyone had been to me, making me feel wanted and welcomed, I still felt like I no longer belonged in Seattle. If I felt that way in a job I really liked, what hope was there for me? My heart was always with you, Dan. And Texas. I was going to come back as soon as I could."

"Wow, really?"

"Yes, I knew I'd never be happy here, while you were there."

"You're a wise woman."

"Glad you noticed."

He laughed and tugged her so they both fell back on the bed. Holding his hand, staring up at the ceiling, all she saw was a bright joy-filled future. Then

Dan took her into his arms and kissed her solidly, reaffirming his love for her.

"I can't wait to marry you, Erin."

"And I can't wait to be your Texas bride."

* * * * *

Don't miss a single installment of the
TEXAS CATTLEMAN'S CLUB: BLACKMAIL
No secret—or heart—is safe in Royal, Texas...

THE TYCOON'S SECRET CHILD
by USA TODAY *bestselling author Maureen Child*

TWO-WEEK TEXAS SEDUCTION
by Cat Schield

REUNITED WITH THE RANCHER
by USA TODAY *bestselling author Sara Orwig*

EXPECTING THE BILLIONAIRE'S BABY
by Andrea Laurence

TRIPLETS FOR THE TEXAN
by USA TODAY *bestselling author Janice Maynard*

A TEXAS-SIZED SECRET
by USA TODAY *bestselling author Maureen Child*

LONE STAR BABY SCANDAL
by Golden Heart winner Lauren Canan

TEMPTED BY THE WRONG TWIN
by USA TODAY *bestselling author Rachel Bailey*

TAKING HOME THE TYCOON
by USA TODAY *bestselling author Catherine Mann*

BILLIONAIRE'S BABY BIND
by USA TODAY *bestselling author*
Katherine Garbera

THE TEXAN TAKES A WIFE
by USA TODAY *bestselling author Charlene Sands*

and

December 2017:
BEST MAN UNDER THE MISTLETOE
by Jules Bennett

***

If you're on Twitter,
tell us what you think of
Harlequin Desire! #harlequindesire

*Can a former bad boy and the woman
he never forgot find true love during one
unforgettable Christmas?
Find out in CHRISTMASTIME COWBOY,
the sizzling new COPPER RIDGE novel from
New York Times bestselling author Maisey Yates.
Read on for your sneak peek...*

LIAM DONNELLY WAS nobody's favorite.

Though being a favorite in their household growing up would never have meant much, Liam was confident that as much as both of his parents disdained their younger son, Alex, they hated Liam more.

And as much as his brothers loved him—or whatever you wanted to call their brand of affection—Liam knew he wasn't the one they'd carry out if there was a house fire. That was fine too.

It wasn't self-pity. It was just a fact.

But while he wasn't anyone's particular favorite, he knew he was at least one person's least favorite.

Sabrina Leighton hated him with every ounce of her beautiful, petite being. Not that he blamed her. But, considering they were having a business meeting today, he did hope that she could keep some of the hatred bottled up.

Liam got out of his truck and put his cowboy hat on, surveying his surroundings. The winery spread was beautiful, with a large, picturesque house over-looking the grounds. The winery and the road leading up to it were carved into an Oregon moun-tainside. Trees and forest surrounded the facility on three sides, creating a secluded feeling. Like the winery was part of another world. In front of the first renovated barn was a sprawling lawn and a path that led down to the river. There was a seating area there and Liam knew that during the warmer months it was a nice place to hang out. Right now, it was too damned cold, and the damp air that blew up from the rushing water sent a chill straight through him.

He shoved his hands in his pockets and kept on walking. There were three rustic barns on the prop-erty that they used for weddings and dinners, and one that had been fully remodeled into a dining and tasting room.

He had seen the new additions online. He hadn't actually been to Grassroots Winery in the past thir-teen years. That was part of the deal. The deal that had been struck back when Jamison Leighton was still owner of the place.

Back when Liam had been nothing more than a good-for-nothing, low-class troublemaker with a couple of misdemeanors to his credit.

Times changed.

Liam might still be all those things at heart, but he was also a successful businessman. And Jamison Leighton no longer owned Grassroots.

Some things, however, hadn't changed. The presence of Sabrina Leighton being one of them.

It had been thirteen years. But he couldn't pretend he thought everything was all right and forgiven. Not considering the way she had reacted when she had seen him at Ace's bar the past few months.

Small towns. Like everybody was at the same party and could only avoid each other for so long.

If it wasn't at the bar, they would most certainly end up at a four-way stop at the same time, or in the same aisle at the grocery store.

But today's meeting would not be accidental. Today's meeting was planned. He wondered if something would get thrown at him. It certainly wouldn't be the first time.

He walked across the gravel lot and into the dining room. It was empty, since the facility—a rustic barn with a wooden chandelier hanging in the center—had yet to open for the day. There was a bar with stools positioned at the front, and tables set up around the room. Back when he had worked here, there had been one basic tasting room, and nowhere for anyone to sit. Most of the wine had been sent out to retail stores for sale, rather than making the winery itself some kind of destination.

He wondered when all of that had changed. He imagined it had something to do with Lindy, the new owner and ex-wife of Jamison Leighton's son, Damien. As far as Liam knew, and he knew enough—considering he didn't get involved with business ventures without figuring out what he was getting into—Damien had drafted the world's dumbest prenuptial agreement. At least, it was dumb for a man who clearly had problems keeping his dick in his pants.

Though why Sabrina was still working at the winery when her sister-in-law had current ownership, and her brother had been deposed, and her parents were—from what he had read in public records—apoplectic about the loss of their family legacy, he didn't know. But he assumed he would find out. At about the same time he found out whether or not something was going to get thrown at his head.

The door from the back opened, and he gritted his teeth. Because, no matter how prepared he felt philosophically to see Sabrina, he knew that there would be impact. There always was. A damned funny thing, that one woman could live in the back of his mind the way she had for so long. That no matter how many years or how many women he put between them, she still burned bright and hot in his memory.

That no matter that he had steeled himself to run into her—because he knew how small towns worked—the impact was like a brick to the side of his head every single time.

She appeared a moment after the door opened, looking severe. Overly so. Her blond hair was pulled back into a high ponytail, and she was wearing a black sheath dress that went down past her knees but conformed to curves that were more generous than they'd been thirteen years ago.

In a good way.

"Hello, Liam," she said, her tone impersonal. Had she not used his first name, it might have been easy to pretend that she didn't know who he was.

"Sabrina."

"Lindy told me that you wanted to talk about a potential joint venture. And since that falls under my jurisdiction as manager of the tasting room, she thought we might want to work together."

Now she was smiling.

The smile was so brittle it looked like it might crack her face.

"Yes, I'm familiar with the details. Particularly since this venture was my idea." He let a small silence hang there for a beat before continuing. "I'm looking at an empty building on the end of Main Street. It would be more than just a tasting room. It would be a small café with some retail space."

"How would it differ from Lane Donnelly's store? She already offers specialty foods."

"Well, we would focus on Grassroots wine and Laughing Irish cheese. Also, I would happily purchase products from Lane's to give the menu a local focus. The café would be nothing big. Just a small lunch place with wine. Very limited selection. Very specialty. But I feel like in a tourist location, that's what you want."

"Great," she said, her smile remaining completely immobile.

He took that moment to examine her more closely. The changes in her face over the years. She was more beautiful now than she had been at seventeen. Her slightly round, soft face had refined in the ensuing years, her cheekbones now more prominent, the angle of her chin sharper.

Her eyebrows looked different too. When she'd been a teenager, they'd been thinner, rounder. Now they were a bit stronger, more angular.

"Great," he returned. "I guess we can go down and have a look at the space sometime this week. Gage West is the owner of the property, and he hasn't listed it yet. Handily, my sister-in-law is good friends with his wife. Both of my sisters-in-law, actually. So I got the inside track on that."

Her expression turned bland. "How impressive."

She sounded absolutely unimpressed. "It wasn't intended to be impressive. Just useful."

She sighed slowly. "Did you have a day of the week in mind to go view the property? Because I really am very busy."

"Are you?"

"Yes," she responded, that smile spreading over her face again. "This is a very demanding job, plus I do have a life."

She stopped short of saying exactly what that life entailed.

"Too busy to do this, which is part of your actual job?" he asked.

On the surface she looked calm, but he could sense a dark energy beneath that spoke of a need to savage him. "I had my schedule sorted out for the next couple of weeks. This is coming together more quickly than expected."

"I'll work something out with Gage and give Lindy a call, how about that?"

"You don't have to call Lindy. I'll give you my phone number. You can call or text me directly."

She reached over to the counter and took a card from the rustic surface, extending her hand toward him. He reached out and took the card, their fingertips brushing as they made the handoff.

And he felt it. Straight down to his groin, where he had always felt things for her, even though it was impossible. Even though he was all wrong for her. And even though now they were doing a business deal together, and she looked like she would cheerfully chew through his flesh if given half the chance.

She might be smiling, but he didn't trust that smile. He was still waiting. Waiting for her to shout recriminations at him now that they were alone. Every other time he had encountered her over the past four months it had been in public. Twice in Ace's bar, and once walking down the street, where she had made a very quick sharp left to avoid walking past him.

It had not been subtle, and it had certainly not spoken of somebody who was over the past.

So his assumption had been that if the two of them were ever alone she was going to let him have it. But she didn't. Instead, she gave him that card and then began to look…bored.

"Did you need anything else?" she asked.

"Not really. Though I have some spreadsheet information that you might want to look over. Ideas that I have for the layout, the menu. It is getting a little ahead of ourselves, in case we end up not liking the venue."

"You've been to look at the venue already, haven't you?" It was vaguely accusatory.

"I have been there, yes. But again, I believe in preparedness. I was hardly going to get very deep into this if I didn't think it was viable. Personally, I'm interested in making sure that we have diverse interests. The economy doesn't typically favor farms, Sabrina. And that is essentially what my brothers and I have. I expect an uphill fight to make that place successful."

She tilted her head to the side. "Like you said, you do your research."

Her friendliness was beginning to slip. And he waited. For something else. For something to get thrown at him. It didn't happen.

"That I do. Take these," he said, handing her the folder that he was holding on to. He made sure their fingers didn't touch this time. "And we'll talk next week."

Then he turned and walked away from her, and he resisted the strong impulse to turn back and get one more glance at her. It wasn't the first time he had resisted that.

He had a feeling it wouldn't be the last.

As soon as Liam walked out of the tasting room, Sabrina let out a breath that had been killing her to keep in. A breath that contained about a thousand insults and recriminations. And more than a few very colorful swear word combinations. A breath that nearly burned her throat, because it was full of so many sharp and terrible things.

She lifted her hands to her face and realized they were shaking. It had been thirteen years. Why did he still affect her like this? Maybe, just maybe, if she had ever found a man who made her feel even half of what Liam did, she wouldn't have such a hard time dealing with him. The feelings wouldn't be so strong.

But she hadn't. So that supposition was basically moot.

The worst part was the tattoos. He'd had about three when he'd been nineteen. Now they covered both of his arms, and she had the strongest urge to make them as familiar to her as the original tattoos had been. To memorize each and every detail about them.

The tree was the one that really caught her attention. The Celtic knots, she knew, were likely a nod to his Irish heritage, but the tree—whose branches she could see stretching down from his shoulder—she was curious about what that meant.

"And you are spending too much time thinking about him," she admonished herself.

She shouldn't be thinking about him at all. She should just focus on congratulating herself for saying nothing stupid. At least she hadn't cried and demanded answers for the night he had completely laid waste to her every feeling.

"How did it go?"

Sabrina turned and saw her sister-in-law, Lindy, come in. People would be forgiven for thinking that she and Lindy were actually biological sisters. In fact, they looked much more alike than Sabrina and her younger sister Beatrix did.

Like Sabrina, Lindy had long, straight blond hair. Bea, on the other hand, had freckles all over her face and a wild riot of reddish-brown curls that resisted taming almost as strongly as the youngest Leighton sibling herself did.

That was another thing Sabrina and Lindy had in common. They were predominantly tame. At least, they kept things as together as they possibly could on the surface.

"Fine."

"You didn't savage him with a cheese knife?"

"Lindy," Sabrina said, "please. This is dry-clean only." She waved her hand up and down, indicating her dress.

"I don't know what your whole issue is with him..."

Because no one spoke of it. Lindy had married Sabrina's brother after the unpleasantness. It was no secret that Sabrina and her father were estranged—even if it was a brittle, quiet estrangement. But unless Damien had told Lindy the details—and

Sabrina doubted he knew all of them—her sister-in-law wouldn't know the whole story.

"I don't have an issue with him," Sabrina said. "I knew him thirteen years ago. That has nothing to do with now. It has nothing to do with this new venture for the winery. Which I am on board with one hundred percent." It was true. She was.

"Well," Lindy said, "that's good to hear."

She could tell that Lindy didn't believe her. "It's going to be fine. I'm looking forward to this." That was also true. Mostly. She was looking forward to expanding Grassroots. Looking forward to helping build the winery, and making it into something that was truly theirs. So that her parents could no longer shout recriminations about Lindy stealing something from the Leighton family.

Eventually, they would make the winery so much more successful that most of it would be theirs.

And if her own issues with her parents were tangled up in all of this, then…that was just how it was.

Sabrina wanted it all to work, and work well. If for no other reason than to prove to Liam Donnelly that she was no longer the seventeen-year-old girl whose world he'd wrecked all those years ago.

In some ways, Sabrina envied the tangible ways in which Lindy had been able to exact revenge on Damien. Of course, Sabrina's relationship with Liam wasn't anything like a ten-year marriage ended by infidelity. She gritted her teeth. She did her best not to think about Liam. About the past. Because it hurt. Every damn time it hurt. It didn't matter if it should or not.

But now that he was back in Copper Ridge, now that she sometimes just happened to run into him, it was worse. It was harder not to think about him.

Him and the grand disaster that had happened after.

* * * * *

Look for CHRISTMASTIME COWBOY,
available from Maisey Yates and HQN Books
wherever books are sold.

COMING NEXT MONTH FROM

HARLEQUIN *Desire*

Available December 5, 2017

#2557 HIS SECRET SON
The Westmoreland Legacy • by Brenda Jackson
The SEAL who fathered Bristol's son died a hero's death...or so she was told. But now Coop is back and vowing to claim his child! Her son deserves to know his father, so Bristol must find a way to fight temptation...and keep her heart safe.

#2558 BEST MAN UNDER THE MISTLETOE
Texas Cattleman's Club: Blackmail • by Jules Bennett
Planning a wedding with the gorgeous, sexy best man would have been a lot easier if he weren't Chelsea Hunt's second-worst enemy. Gabe Walsh is furious that the sins of his uncle have also fallen on him, but soon his desire to prove his innocence turns into the desire to make her his!

#2559 THE CHRISTMAS BABY BONUS
Billionaires and Babies • by Yvonne Lindsay
Getting snowed in with his sexy assistant is difficult enough. But when an abandoned baby is found in the stables, die-hard bachelor Piers may find himself yearning for a family for Christmas...

#2560 LITTLE SECRETS: HIS PREGNANT SECRETARY
Little Secrets • by Joanne Rock
After a heated argument with his secretary turns sexually explosive, entrepreneur Jager McNeill knows the right thing to do is propose... because now she's carrying his child! But what will he do when she won't settle for a marriage of convenience?

#2561 SNOWED IN WITH A BILLIONAIRE
Secrets of the A-List • by Karen Booth
Joy McKinley just *had* to be rescued by one of the wealthiest, sexiest men she's ever met. Especially when she's hiding out in someone else's house under a name that isn't hers. But when they get snowed in together, can their romance survive the truth?

#2562 BABY IN THE MAKING
Accidental Heirs • by Elizabeth Bevarly
Surprise heir Hannah Robinson will lose her fortune if she doesn't get pregnant. Enter daredevil entrepreneur Yeager Novak...and the child they'll make together! Opposites attract on this baby-making adventure, but will that be enough to turn their pact into a real romance?

HDCNM1117

Get 2 Free Books,

Plus 2 Free Gifts—

just for trying the Reader Service!

HARLEQUIN *Desire*

YES! Please send me 2 FREE Harlequin® Desire novels and my 2 FREE gifts (gifts are worth about $10 retail). After receiving them, if I don't wish to receive any more books, I can return the shipping statement marked "cancel." If I don't cancel, I will receive 6 brand-new novels every month and be billed just $4.55 per book in the U.S. or $5.24 per book in Canada. That's a savings of at least 13% off the cover price! It's quite a bargain! Shipping and handling is just 50¢ per book in the U.S. and 75¢ per book in Canada.* I understand that accepting the 2 free books and gifts places me under no obligation to buy anything. I can always return a shipment and cancel at any time. The free books and gifts are mine to keep no matter what I decide.

225/326 HDN GMRV

Name	(PLEASE PRINT)

Address	Apt. #

City	State/Prov.	Zip/Postal Code

Signature (if under 18, a parent or guardian must sign)

Mail to the **Reader Service:**
IN U.S.A.: P.O. Box 1341, Buffalo, NY 14240-8531
IN CANADA: P.O. Box 603, Fort Erie, Ontario L2A 5X3

Want to try two free books from another line?
Call 1-800-873-8635 or visit www.ReaderService.com.

*Terms and prices subject to change without notice. Prices do not include applicable taxes. Sales tax applicable in N.Y. Canadian residents will be charged applicable taxes. Offer not valid in Quebec. This offer is limited to one order per household. Books received may not be as shown. Not valid for current subscribers to Harlequin Desire books. All orders subject to approval. Credit or debit balances in a customer's account(s) may be offset by any other outstanding balance owed by or to the customer. Please allow 4 to 6 weeks for delivery. Offer available while quantities last.

Your Privacy—The Reader Service is committed to protecting your privacy. Our Privacy Policy is available online at www.ReaderService.com or upon request from the Reader Service.

We make a portion of our mailing list available to reputable third parties that offer products we believe may interest you. If you prefer that we not exchange your name with third parties, or if you wish to clarify or modify your communication preferences, please visit us at www.ReaderService.com/consumerchoice or write to us at Reader Service Preference Service, P.O. Box 9062, Buffalo, NY 14240-9062. Include your complete name and address.

HD17R2

*Bane Westmoreland's SEAL team is made up of
sexy alpha males.*

*Don't miss Laramie "Coop" Cooper's story
HIS SECRET SON
from New York Times bestselling author Brenda Jackson!*

*The SEAL who fathered Bristol's son died a hero's death...or
so she was told. But now Coop is back and vowing to claim
his child! Her son deserves to know his father, so Bristol must
find a way to fight temptation...and keep her heart safe.*

*Read on for a sneak peek at
HIS SECRET SON,
part of THE WESTMORELAND LEGACY series.*

Laramie stared at Bristol. "You were pregnant?"

"Yes," she said in a soft voice. "And you're free to order a
paternity test if you need to verify that my son is yours."

He had a son? It took less than a second for his emotions to
go from shock to disbelief. "How?"

She lifted a brow. "Probably from making love almost
nonstop for three solid days."

They had definitely done that. Although he'd used a condom
each and every time, he knew there was always a possibility
that something could go wrong.

"And where is he?" he asked.

"At home."

Where the hell was that? It bothered him how little he knew about the woman who'd just announced she'd given birth to his child. At least she'd tried contacting him to let him know. Some women would not have done so.

If his child had been born nine months after their holiday fling, that meant he would have turned two in September. While Laramie was in a cell, somewhere in the world, Bristol had been giving life.

To his child.

Emotions Laramie had never felt before suddenly bombarded him with the impact of a Tomahawk missile. He was a parent, which meant he had to think about someone other than himself. He wasn't sure how he felt about that. But then, wasn't he used to taking care of others as a member of his SEAL team?

She nodded. "I'm not asking you for anything Laramie, if that's what you're thinking. I just felt you had a right to know about the baby."

She wasn't asking him for anything? Did she not know her bold declaration that he'd fathered her child demanded everything?

"I want to see him."

"You will. I would never keep Laramie from you."

"You named him Laramie?" Even more emotions swamped him. Her son—their son—had his name?

She hesitated. "Yes."

Then he asked, "So, what's your reason for giving yourself my last name, as well?"

Don't miss
HIS SECRET SON
by New York Times *bestselling author Brenda Jackson,*
available December 2017
wherever Harlequin® Desire books and ebooks are sold.

www.Harlequin.com

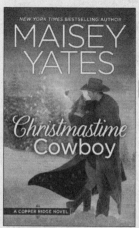

LOVE
Harlequin
romance?

Join our Harlequin community to share your thoughts and connect with other romance readers!

Be the first to find out about promotions, news, and exclusive content!

Sign up for the Harlequin e-newsletter and download a free book from any series at

www.TryHarlequin.com

CONNECT WITH US AT:

Harlequin.com/Community

 Facebook.com/HarlequinBooks

 Twitter.com/HarlequinBooks

 Instagram.com/HarlequinBooks

 Pinterest.com/HarlequinBooks

ReaderService.com

**ROMANCE WHEN
YOU NEED IT**

HSOCIAL2017